ALLEGEDLY

ALLEGEDLY

"The Diary of a Prison Wife"

JESSICA HAYS

Trendstar Publishing

ALLEGEDLY: THE DIARY OF A PRISON WIFE
BY JESSICA HAYS

Editing and Interior Layout by TRENDSTAR PUBLISHING

First Printing, 2024

ISBN 978 - 1 - 737524 - 85 - 4

This novel is a work of fiction. Any references to real people, family, events, establishments, or locales are intended to give the story a sense of reality and authenticity. Other names, places, characters, brands, companies, and any incidents occurring in the works are either the product of the author's imagination or are used fictitiously.

Published by:

TRENDSTAR PUBLISHING LLC

2875 S Orange Ave Ste 500-6735
Orlando, FL, 32805

support@trendstarbooks.com www.trendstarbooks.com

I dedicate this book to my mother. Mom, I don't even know where to begin. You're an angel on earth, and I am so blessed to have you as my mother. Even though you struggled as a single mother, you made it your duty never to let me see that. All I saw was a strong, independent, and fun woman. I only hope I can be half the mother you are. Thank you for ALWAYS having my back and being my most extensive support system. Without you, I don't know where I would be. You are my number one, my best friend, and the person I have always been able to count on. Thank you, Mommy. I am truly grateful.

Contents

I

The Foundation

Growing up, my mom always told me to marry and date a man with money. She should have told me to make my own, but I took her advice in my way. We can call it bad advice or daddy issues, but I had an interesting type in men. I am one of those women who always thought a man could be saved. Well, this boyfriend was like the previous ones. He had a lot of money, sold drugs, was 100% Colombian, 320 pounds, and was a 6'4' bodybuilder. I had to have him! Boy, was I a sucker for a powerful man - especially one that speaks Spanish—a man who made me feel so special while making everyone else feel so small. Let's just say we hit it off. Marco had contacted me on social media for about a year, once or twice. However, I had a boyfriend at the time. That relationship didn't last long, and I eventually responded to Marco. That same day, he came over with a "goodie bag." You can guess what that means. I lived with my mother then, and as laid back as she was, she still had her boundaries. Yeah, I smoked weed and took anxiety medication, but this goodie bag had other stuff in it. Good, but bad.

In the days that followed, Marco and I were having a blast, going for walks, talking about life, and enjoying each other's company. One day, we walked home and entered my room, only for my mom to follow us and find a pile of pure cocaine sitting on my dresser. She was furious! Right before us, she flushed the coke in the toilet, which cost about $800. Allegedly. Anyhow, we just continued with our day. There was something different about him. Usually, I would get sick of men and could only stand to be around them in small doses. But I didn't want Marco to leave.

I wanted him to stay and never go. Call it love at first sight or soul mates, but we saw each other daily for I don't know how many months. The passion and chemistry were unreal on both ends. No, we did not continue to do the coke. At the time, Marco only sold weed, allegedly. Marco and I were inseparable. We did everything together. He was like a father to my 3-year-old daughter, Lucy, of whom I had 50/50 custody at the time. We fell so in love, just rolling around on the floor, loving and exploring each other. Eventually, we wanted a child of our own. We didn't "plan" it but weren't preventing it. Well, it worked. I got pregnant. I was so excited I thought I would give him the positive pregnancy test inside a Build-A-Bear dog and then give it to him the same day. He opened the box and about cried. My mom was with me the whole time and was a massive support system.

We were thrilled, over the moon, to have a little us running around soon. I stopped everything unhealthy and started eating right. About three days after confirming the pregnancy, I started to bleed. Yep, I began miscarrying. It was one of the worst days of my life (during this time in my life). We went back to the doctor, and they sat me down to do the ultrasound. They could no longer find the baby's heartbeat. Marco and I were devastated. It got to the point where it began to ruin our relationship. Day by day, things kept getting worse. I was so depressed I was overdoing my anxiety medication. Marco was so depressed he began to neglect and ignore me. The only thing keeping us together was the sex. It was ALWAYS amazing. TMI, I know. But it played a big part in our relationship. Well, amid our loss and most likely breakup, I got pregnant again. This time, I didn't miscarry. Marco didn't think the baby was his because we had just broken up and been on the rocks before that. I understood, but I wouldn't say I liked it at all. Marco wasn't just big; he was enormous, not just because he worked out daily. He was also huge due to the number of steroids he was using. Ever heard of "roid rage?" It's a real thing. Throughout my pregnancy, I had to deal with Marcos's sporadic roid rage incidents that all revolved around me. There would be points where I would have to turn off my phone to avoid being called a slut or a whore.

I would often run to the house of one of my best friends of 23 years to get away from it all. The toxicity became a habit. However, Brianna was a person who was always there when I needed a place to run to. She also had a daughter, Violet, who got along with Lucy great, which made it easier for us to hang out, as they would entertain each other. Not only that, but she was also pregnant with a little boy whom she named Ben. We were only two weeks apart from each other. The circumstances made it easy for us to bond because we both had to follow the same rules. I can't tell you how often I ran to her house because Marco didn't know where she lived, so he couldn't just "show up." Brianna saved me many times and continued to do so into the future.

It is safe to say that my pregnancy was awful. Not just because of Marco but also because I suffered from morning sickness every single day. So much so that I only gained twenty-two pounds with her at the end of my pregnancy. Mind you, I am tall and skinny.

Furthermore, the day came when it was time to have our daughter, Lexi. Being that I am so small, I must have C-sections to ensure the safety of myself and the baby. She was born in February of 2017. I always knew she was Marco's because I knew I didn't cheat or sleep with anyone else while single. No need to. Marco, however, always second-guessed it. He was with me the day she was born. For me, it was one of the best days of my life. Unfortunately, Marco was still skeptical.

2

The Transition

The day came when I got to take Lexi home to my mother's house, which was beautiful. It is a sound 3,000 square feet with a screened-in pool, five bedrooms, two living rooms, a loft, and a beautiful layout. The kids had joined rooms with a bathroom in between. I was thrilled to have my beautiful girls in my house, but Marco was not yet present.

Marco once told me, "I need this paternity test before we get serious about this."

I said, "That's no problem."

He wanted a DNA test to ensure that Lexi was his. I encouraged it, as I already knew the answer to the results. He came over, and we did the whole swabs and all. As I continued caring for Lexi, we waited for the results. They came back positive, and Marco was beyond happy, but I just wanted to rub it in his face. He came right over with a big wad of money and arms wide open.

He told me, "I can't believe I'm a father. Thank you so much, Jessie."

He was so cute, being so big, holding that tiny baby. Imagine this vast man, scary and dangerous, loving on this little innocent child. It was one of the sweetest things I think I've experienced. He fell in love immediately. He may not have been the best to me, but boy, was he a fantastic father to both of my children. His biggest concern was being a provider to me and the girls, so he wanted to make more money. He did not care how he did that as long as he made money. Now, Marco already had a felony for something violent. Granted, it was just a fight, but Marco had put the other person into a coma due to the battle, leaving him with permanent disfiguration of the face. Since the kid was in a coma, the parents pressed charges to the maximum extent.

The kid had stolen Marcos's friend's iPod, leading to the fight that led to his charges. This charge on his record made it impossible for him to get a job anywhere, and the situation made Marco want to make money in other ways. He was already making money selling excessive amounts of weed, allegedly, but wanted more. He intended for the kids to have more, for me to have more, to spoil us all, and to put a roof over our heads, precisely what he did. Allegedly, he began to sell cocaine and upped his salary by a landslide. He was set!

As that year went by, Marco and I grew closer again. I still had trust issues. Knowing what he did for a living, I wasn't ready to move in with him and the children yet. But then, Marco began to become the man I always wanted him to be. He came over all the time to see me and the children, and this goes without saying, but he took care of us financially. He went above and beyond with the whole financial part of the relationship.

Marco would tell me, "I don't want you working. I want you home with the children. They should be raised by their mother."

He felt very strongly about this. By the end of the year, Marco had rented a house with a fenced-in backyard and three bedrooms. It was adorable. But I was still weary and needed clarification on whether he wanted us to move in or if I even wanted to move in.

Eventually, he approached me and said, "Why haven't you moved in yet? I have it all set up for a family and am ready to make that jump."

Given some of his recent behavior, I explained that I wasn't sure if he really wanted us to move in. He would have mood swings because of the steroids, which made it difficult for me to see the amount of love he carried for me. Our good times were great, our tough times were horrible. But we will get to that later.

Lexi was about a year old when we all moved into Marco's new house that he got for us. When we first moved in, it felt like a fairy tale. Everything was exactly how I pictured: eating family dinners, playing games, inflatable pools in the backyard, and everything a family does. Something you dream about as a child. That is precisely how your family is supposed to be. But as time went on, Marco began to get more comfortable and much more prominent. I was running out of things to cook and games to play. I could not keep up with the lifestyle that Marco was providing. It included cleaning up until 3 am some nights to keep up with the house, the animals, and Marco's eating habits.

Given Marco's alleged "profession," it would tend to give him specific things to be mad about. However, I was the only person he had to take his anger out on. As time went on, things got worse. Each argument became worse than the last. I loved Marco, and despite our arguments worsening, we still had good and great times. We had enough money to do whatever we liked. Living in Orlando, Florida, the options for different things to do were limitless, which helped us during our tough times or turned good ones into great ones. I was so indecisive as to what to do. He was then the father of my child, the man of my dreams, but with an explosive and unpredictable temper. A regular day jackal and hide. I continued.

I enjoyed the great times intently and dealt with the troubled times accordingly. By accordingly, I mean quietly. I would not yell back, I would not talk back, I would wait for it to end. These spur-of-the-moment outbursts would last about 20 to 30 minutes, and he would apologize until he was blue. I would always accept his apology three days later. I didn't think the arguments could get any worse. The verbal abuse was taking a toll on my mental health and personal well-being. I no longer felt like myself. I didn't know who that person was anymore. As the fighting continued, it escalated from not just verbal abuse but physical abuse. Being as small as I am, about one hundred pounds, this complicated things. Not only was my mental health being affected, but safety was now in question. I no longer felt safe where I slept. Granted, this never happened to or around the children (thank goodness), but this was my reality, with no way out. If I went to my mother's house, he would follow. If I went to friends, I put them and their families in danger, and I was NOT about to put Brianna in that situation. So, I bit the bullet for a good 6 to 7 months of abuse. It wasn't constant, but it was enough to destroy me. I lost myself in continual fear. I stopped talking, which was mistaken for awkwardness or like I was "hiding" something.

Along came Christmas, and I was so excited to spend the day with my kids, watching them open their thousands of dollars worth of toys and games, the little smiles on their faces as they ripped through the wrapping paper. With this being the BIGGEST Christmas I've ever experienced, I didn't realize how much time and effort went into wrapping and organizing all these presents. I stayed up all night wrapping Christmas presents, and Marco fell asleep after a binder. A binder is where he would stay up all night trying out his alleged "product." Doing this did not help his temper, and I knew it, but I couldn't tell him anything without him getting upset. So, I let him sleep as I went to work on putting toys together, wrapping toys, and organizing them under the tree to make sure the kids had the best Christmas ever! But that wasn't t the case.

I had bit off more than I could chew, and by the time I had wrapped the presents and placed them under the tree, it was about 6 am. Granted, I had taken Adderall to stay awake and get the tremendous amount of Christmas wrapping done, but I fell asleep on the couch hard that morning. I couldn't do it.

I woke up to Marcos's mom poking me, saying, "Jessica, wake up. It's Christmas!" I quickly got up, panicked, and looked for the kids. They were fine and still asleep, as was Marco.

Marco's mom, Olga, said, "Jessica, go wake up Marco. We are going to start making dinner soon".

As she encouraged me to wake him up, I felt horrible. I still waited about 30 minutes before attempting to wake him up, being weary, knowing he needed as much sleep as he could get. And needed to be woken up to food already made, not to watch food get made. Remember his size! He had to eat like that to gain muscle, which stretched his stomach to the point that he was always hungry and always had to eat. Well, more of his family kept showing up and told me to wake him up, so I began going in and waking him up slowly, and as he got up, he stumbled. I was worried and didn't know how to shield this from his entire family on Christmas, so I got his cousin, who already knew what was happening without judgment. He took it upon himself to get Marco out of bed and dressed. Marco was NOT happy. I was with his cousin's wife in the kitchen, helping with dinner, when he left our room and entered the dining room.

Once Marco walked into the dining room, he made direct eye contact with me, giving me a stare I had unfortunately become familiar with. I began to get nervous and tried to stay busy in the kitchen, but he kept staring. The kids started to open their presents. They loved them and had a blast while I was sweating bullets, thinking about what would happen to me once all his family members left. I was stunned! This was my favorite day of the year since I was a little girl. Now, getting to watch my little girls open their presents every year. However, this Christmas was different. I wasn't happy. I wasn't smiling, I was sweating. I looked horrible, felt horrible, all awful emotions. Not ones I am used to feeling on Christmas day.

Once the kids opened their presents, dinner was ready, and everyone sat at our dinner table to eat. Marco was sitting on the other side of the table from where I was, and he gave me that familiar stare and didn't break eye contact. I continued to look down and pick at my food (which he hated when I did that) and pray that he would snap out of it before everyone left. As people started to go, I began to freak out, considering what I thought/knew was in store for my future. I began begging his cousin to take us with them or not to leave me there with Marco. Although, I don't think he believed me. So, I then turned to his mother, feeling her maternal instincts would kick in, but I was wrong. As I explained, crying, to please not leave me alone, she said I would be fine, and it would all work out. Boy, was she wrong! Marco's cousin's wife, Cicci, was the only person by my side willing not to leave. She believed me. She stayed by my side and said she wouldn't leave, but I didn't want to put her in the middle of whatever was about to happen. Therefore, I asked her to go with her family and that I would be okay. Eventually, after some convincing, Cicci left, and I was alone. The kids were playing with their new toys, and the next thing I knew, I was on the ground. I had been kicked with sneakers and slammed on the floor. All this occurred in the bedroom, so the kids saw nothing. I'm not saying that it wasn't traumatizing for me. I got up and didn't know what happened. I had a concussion because I was so confused as to if I got hurt or not, but my ribs and chest were in a lot of pain.

I sat at the dining room table, trying to put the pieces together, while my kids sat in the living room, no longer playing with their toys. They must have heard something (at least my oldest daughter) and realized something wasn't right. She stayed quiet and patient.

Marco said to me, "Call the police if you want to. I'm going to bed."

I waited and finally put everything together—everything that happened and why. I was in pain. I waited patiently until I thought he was in a deep sleep. Once I heard the snoring, I waited about 30 minutes, and with those 30 minutes, I packed a bag with everything I could fit for the kids. I told Lucy to grab whatever she could hold, and that's all we were bringing. It broke my heart after watching them open all their Christmas presents and watching them forced to leave them all behind the same night. Lucy chose to bring her three favorite cat stuffed animals that she had forever and nothing else. I had her watch her sister while I ensured Marco was fully asleep. I went into "our" room and grabbed his prescription of Xanax, then continued to shake it and see if the noise stopped his snoring. It didn't. He didn't wake up. I then ran, grabbed the kids and the bag, and went through the garage because the front door would notify him on his phone if it opened or closed. We ran to my car. Lucy got Lexi into her car seat, and we hit the road. As I am driving, I realize how bad my injuries are. I parked in a Walmart parking lot across from my mother's house, and a police car pulled up. I thought it must be fate that this happened for a reason, and I needed to make sure that my lungs weren't punctured. I got transported by ambulance as my kids were in the ambulance with me to the closest hospital. We got to the hospital, and they immediately did x-rays and saw that I had two broken ribs and a chest contusion (bruising of the chest). Once I received this information, I was done. I was done with Marco and had to get as far away as possible so he could not get to me and the children.

3

The Run

Realizing I had no money for gas and food to make it to my grand-parents' house in West Virginia, the hospital provided us with a place to go where no one would find me or the kids. It was a place for victims of domestic violence. The place was so secret that they would not give anyone the address. They met us at a 7-eleven gas station near the shelter and had us follow them there. The maneuver prevented any-one from finding anyone, let alone me and the girls. I knew he would look first at my mother's house. And I wasn't wrong. That was his first stop once he woke up from his slumber and saw that I was no longer in the house and had taken the kids. While he realized how badly he messed up, I was busy getting to the women's protective shelter with my children until I could go to my mother's job to ask her for enough money to get to West Virginia and ensure she told Marco nothing. I thought he had a tracker on my phone, so I chucked it out the window on my way to the shelter and used my daughter Lucy's phone to reach my mother and grandpa to let them know I was on the move with the kids. My grandad was over the moon when he heard that we were coming. However, I wasn't. I was worried and injured. Early the next day, we went to see my mother at work.

Once there, she said, "Here, take my debit card and some cash to get you three up North to Pappy's. I won't tell anyone where you are."

"Thank you so much mom!" I replied.

See, my grandpa lives in the middle of nowhere. He lives between Ohio and Pennsylvania in the northern panhandle of West Virginia. He owns fourteen acres of land with a half-mile-long driveway, no neighbors, it is almost impossible to find. You couldn't find it if you tried your best to. West Virginia it was, the day after Christmas, with two children, two broken ribs, and a chest contusion. I knew that it was going to be a long drive. My mother gave me the money around 4:00 pm, and I was rushing to leave before Marco caught on. I stopped at Publix and got the essentials for me and the kids, filled up my gas tank, and then went on my journey around 6:00 pm. Therefore, I was about to drive all night until I got to West Virginia from Florida. So, I began moving across the country to ensure our safety. I drove all night, occasionally stopping at rest stops to take naps, ensuring we got there safely. The good thing about driving through the night is the kids were asleep most of the way, and there was no traffic, so I didn't mind it (other than my ribs hurting). After naps and driving all night long, I made it. I made it to my grandparents' house! The kids were thrilled, and it was a total culture shock as we went from Central Florida to the middle of nowhere, West Virginia.

4

West Virginia

After driving all night, we arrived early the next morning. The kids woke up rested and ready for a day of exploring. Unfortunately, with my ribs broken, I couldn't even pick up my 3-year-old daughter. I needed time to recover physically and to spend catching up with my grandpa. Hanging out with him was easy. I didn't have to do much of anything. With no way for Marco to contact me, I had two weeks of peace and silence as I recovered from my injuries. We organized the basement (with a bedroom). Weeks later, I began responding to Marco's text once he realized I was using Lucy's phone. Frankly, I let him have it, knowing I was 1,800 miles away. I vented, spoke the truth about how he treated me and went into extreme detail about why I left.

Surprisingly, one day, he apologized and said, "I will do anything to have my family back."

As badly as I wanted to believe him, I had to wait as long as possible and see how willing he was to change. I pushed every button he had, told him I hated him for how he treated me and called him so many names that I don't even remember most of them. I tested him relentlessly and got my anger out in the process. Doing this helped me feel better and get things I had been holding in for so many months out. I got him to start taking bipolar medication. In the meantime, I was stuck in West Virginia for months during the worst winter in 30 years. Being born and raised in Florida, snow was a new ball game for me. From driving in it to times when we could not leave the house to get groceries. My kids were constantly getting sick, so I had to keep them inside as much as possible, which became very dull after a certain amount of time. Most of the time, pizza couldn't even be delivered to the house because of the snow. It was hell! But it was still better to rest and recover than to clean the entire house and care for animals. Honestly, the first three months were my most relaxing time in years. The kids were good. I could relax and not clean constantly, as no animals were in the house. I could finally catch up on my TV shows and spend personal time with the children. But after that 3-month mark, things began to get very restless.

My mother visited me, and we decided it would be a clever idea to get a dog to keep me busy, a therapy dog from the shelter. We went to a shelter in Ohio to see what kind of dogs they had to offer. When we arrived, we looked at all the older dogs in the shelter, as we did not want a puppy. But there was this dog that caught my eye. I am a vet tech and have always told myself I would never own a German Shepherd. I was wrong. I fell in love with this dog as he was sweet, playful, a year old, and gorgeous. All the markings of a German Shepherd other than the black "muzzle." We adopted him and named him Apache. We brought him home, but he was still so young that he didn't do as well with my grandfather as we had hoped. However, Apache LOVED the farm. He was always running and playing, often getting ticks all over him. My mother and I constantly had to take him 45 minutes to another state to get him professionally groomed. West Virginia wasn't the friendliest in terms of resources being close by. Nevertheless, Apache helped me and my family tremendously when it came to our mental health.

When we arrived in West Virginia, we had nothing: no toys, no clothes, shit, no underwear. I used my mom's card to get the essentials, and my grandpa helped me. However, I still needed toys for the kids to play with. Growing up, I would visit West Virginia every summer for 2 to 3 months to see my grandparents. Well, I had begun laying down roots there and making friends. Making friends here was easy. The town was so small that everyone knew everyone. I had plenty of friends there growing up. But as we got older, more and more of my friends from West Virginia started to pass away. They were passing away from things like car accidents and drug overdoses. But one friend of mine maintained and didn't get into the whole "junkie" scene. Her name was Bethany. The first day I was in West Virginia, I called Bethany to let her know I would be staying at my grandparents' house for a while and asked if she wanted a play date because she had two children. She had one girl around nine and a little boy around two. She loved the idea, and we made plans to see each other the next day. Little did I know, she was only a few miles away from us, on the same main road. We got to her house, and I explained what I was dealing with to her and her husband.

I told them, "I'm running from Marco and staying here until I feel safe."

"Oh my God," said Bethany.

They knew I had nothing but the clothes on my back, so Bethany went through all her kids' old clothes and toys and packed my car with everything we could need. It was the sweetest gesture ever. The things she gave us got us through that first month. We continued to hang out as often as possible, as much as her job would allow. She had always been a great friend, but this was huge.

Financially, Marco supported us for the six months that we were away, hoping that it would show me that he would keep me no matter the situation or how badly I yelled and cursed at him, which helped. He would call daily, even knowing he may get screamed at from the other end. I was still mad, rightfully. I told his whole family and friends I no longer cared during the beginning. As time went on, however, I began to miss Marco. Again, he was becoming the man I fell in love with many years ago. Lucy also started to miss him and wanted to have her upcoming birthday party in Florida with Marco. Seeing this touched my heart to the fullest, and I honestly felt the same. I spent about a month of consideration as to what I should do. If I went back, I would still take the chance of history repeating itself, or I could have my fairy tale ending. It was a 50/50 chance that one of these two situations would occur. However, I took my chances. I was so in love with Marco and missed his big arms wrapped around me. Being that I stayed across the country for six months, got him on medication to help with the mood swings, and showed him that I was not playing around and would leave if need be. He realized how important family was in this dramatic event that we went through. So, the month of Lucy's birthday, we began packing all our belongings gathered during our stay in West Virginia. I also decided to take the journey at night again. However, I felt uncomfortable leaving with my grandpa in his old age. He lived alone once my grandma was put into a nursing home, which he visited every day, snow, or shine. He never missed a day. It was a "Notebook" kind of love. My grandma was diagnosed with dementia, and my grandpa hasn't left her side since. Also, he was away often, leaving Apache unattended and stuck in the house. Apache was still in the puppy stage and needed to run and get his energy out. If not, he would usually begin to act up.

I decided to bring Apache back to Florida with us, knowing that Marco had a 160-pound Rottweiler, who was not the friendliest with new people or animals. I still wanted to introduce them properly. Marco and I discussed it and agreed that Apache should come along. After a long 2 to 3 days of packing in West Virginia, we had loaded up the car and were ready to go. I ensured I slept during the day to drive safely at night with two kids and a German Shepherd. I wasn't thrilled, but I hoped for a relaxing ride once the kids were asleep. Around 6:30 pm, I got the kids and Apache into the car, said goodbye to my grandpa, and left on my road trip back to Orlando, Florida.

5

Back To Florida

The trip started with Lexi throwing up all over herself, as she suffered from motion sickness, and let's say West Virginia's roads aren't on the straight and narrow. I pulled over immediately, changed her, and threw away the messed-up clothes as I couldn't have them in the car the whole ride! We began again on our adventure. Apache was not a dog that barked. I had only heard him bark when someone arrived at the house. As we continued to drive, it got darker, as expected, and the roads were still windy. As I was going, I couldn't see much because there were no streetlights. It's a good thing Apache could. I noticed he began to bark for the first time, and I started to try to figure out what he was barking at in front of me. Apache began to bark louder as we continued, and then I saw it. There was a deer directly in front of me. Some may say this was a coincidence, but he saved our lives that night, as I would not have been looking for anything had he not been barking. It's safe to say that he was MY dog after that moment. I fully trusted him and knew he was intelligent enough to watch out for us.

After about 11 hours of driving, we arrived in Florida. Man, it was great to smell the ocean and see the palm trees again in the lovely, warm weather, unlike West Virginia's freezing air and snow. I was delighted to be back and to restart my life with Marco, the kids, and the dogs. We finally pulled into Marco's new town-home, and it was adorable. Perfect for our family! When Marco opened the door, I felt like a little kid with butterflies again. We gave each other the biggest hug and so many kisses. We missed each other so much! To be reunited was a fantastic experience. The children were beyond happy and excited to be at their new house, with their rooms and TVs and having their dad back. Everyone was delighted, but there was still so much to do when it came to unpacking AND shopping for toys for the kids' rooms and downstairs living room. Marco had already set up their bed and TVs before we arrived. We just needed to add toys and decorations to make it feel more like home. We also had another dog, Baxter, a Chiweenie, which you will learn about soon. I've never met a dog with a better personality than Baxter.

Once we moved in and new furniture arrived, we began to look more and more like a family and our house more like a home. We were doing all types of stuff as a family. Sine family to Marco was now everything. He began putting us first, before his alleged work, ensuring we spent every moment together. And I mean every moment. As he provided, I cared for the family and planned little adventures. Everything was normal, not just average, but too good to be true. Unfortunately, this phase only lasted a good **five** months before things began to get rocky and took a turn for the worse. Granted, it was the first incident since I had returned from West Virginia, but I was not allowing it. One day, Marco got mad at me, overthinking that I was somewhere I said I wasn't, which wasn't true. He pulled a "Marco" and began to yell at me threateningly. I was done allowing him to treat me like this. Lucy was in school, and Lexi was taking a nap while all this was happening. I knew Marco had a friend coming by, so as he was getting dressed, so was I. I packed a bag for Lucy and myself and waited patiently for Marco's friend to show up, as I knew Marco wouldn't do anything in front of his friend that would cause him to be judged. Finally, the moment arrived when his friend showed up.

Once I heard that door open, I ran downstairs with Lexi and went straight for the front door. But when he realized what was happening, he wouldn't let me leave until I calmed down, which was understandable as I was crying hysterically and probably shouldn't have been driving. He eventually got me to calm down, apologized for his behavior, and said he would do his best to ensure it didn't happen again. I gave him another chance and came back inside with Lexi. It completely ruined my day, but at least he knew what he was up against if he mistreated me. I would not be aggressive towards him, but I was willing to leave at any moment if not treated right. It worked, as the next couple of months were amazing. We were so in love with each other and our adorable little family. We had it all: love, family, money and more. All the things that are essential in this so-called life. Marco treated us like princesses, emotionally and financially. Whenever we went out, we could buy the best of the best, meaning new sunglasses for me, toys, and enormous doughnuts for the kids. We would always be wearing matching Jordans like we were the cutest couple ever.

6

The New Start

The holidays came around, and believe it or not, I was thrilled! Knowing how our relationship has grown and how bonded our family has become. Thank goodness, it was Thanksgiving! We decided to have Marco's cousin and wife cook for everyone since they are professional chefs. I'm not the best cook, but those two could make magic in the kitchen. Trust me, that's not the only reason we invited them over. They were some of our closest friends. Marco's cousin's wife, Cecelia (Cici), was my best friend. She was always there for me, even during my West Virginia trip. While I was up there recovering, she flew up to West Virginia to help me with the kids and get settled in due to my ribs. She stayed for a few weeks, and at this point in my life, I don't know what I would have done without her. She flew up during one of the worst winters in 30 years to sit with me at my grandparents' house. We were so close. Anyhow, let's get back to Thanksgiving with all six of us. This Thanksgiving was relaxing, and the food was delicious. We would frequently go out back and smoke, come in with red eyes and a hungry belly. Everything felt right. Once dinner was over, we watched a movie, and then our guests headed home. It was drama-free, relaxing, and fun all day. I was warm and cozy inside, and we ended the night by playing a game and going to bed. From Thanksgiving to Christmas, it had been super quiet and peaceful. Even though the peace did not last long, it was the best year of my life. I felt like myself, free and complete. We were then going into Halloween. The girls were so excited. Lucy would be the Queen of Hearts, and Lexi would be Tinker Bell. The neighborhood where Marco and I lived wasn't the most "kid-friendly" neighborhood you could live in. Fortunately, my mother lives in a very family-friendly neighborhood, where most people work at Disney and have a family. People went "all out" with decorations, such as people in cages as you walked up to their front door. It was an incredible event, so we took the girls to my mother's house to trick-or-treat. It was so much fun! We covered ourselves in bug spray to stay out and get as much candy as possible! We were professionals. We used pillowcases instead of Halloween bags, then brought extra pillowcases to empty the full ones into. I thought it was genius, and the kids got so much candy! After we were done trick-or-treating, we returned to my mom's house, let the kids dump their candies on the table, and started eating! Well, after I checked the ones they wanted, I gave it to them. You never know what could be in those candies, so I always look to ensure they aren't open or suspicious. Once the kids had their fair share of candy, they packed their pillowcases, and we headed home. Getting them to sleep that night was a nightmare!

Along came Christmas, and Marco was hustling more than ever to ensure he could get everyone everything they wanted. Extremely sweet but dangerous, allegedly. There was a time when he handed me a backpack and asked me how much I thought was in there. It was so heavy I couldn't even guess. Anyhow, that was our Christmas money. Let me tell you, that was a Christmas to remember for all of us. Not only were we so financially stable, but we were in the best place in our relationship that we had ever been. The Christmas spirit was in the air, the cookies, Santa, putting up and decorating the tree. All these things made me so happy. I decorated the whole house and ensured I started wrapping days early this time so we didn't have another mishap. Everything was going according to plan.

I began ordering presents around Halloween to ensure they arrived on time. I even got Marco to fit his massive ass into a Christmas Grinch onesie! It was their largest one, and he still needed to work to get into it. I laughed so hard that my Apple watch fell off my wrist and smashed on the tile. I went from laughing to crying. My watch was super important, so Marco bought me a new one. Problem solved. We see my mother every Christmas at her house, but she came to our house with a TRUNK full of toys this Christmas. That's not including what Marco and I got the kids. It took them forever to open all their presents. It was the best Christmas of my life.

7

Lucy

Once we settled after Christmas, Marco and I decided to have another baby. Another addition to the family, as we could afford it and were in a great place in our relationship. After our conversation about it, I decided to get my IUD removed and begin to add to our family. I had it removed right after Christmas, and from there, the fun began. We tried for about a month. However, some unfortunate events that would change our lives forever happened within that month. When I met Marco before Lexi, I only knew what he did for a living once I was already head over heels for him, and what he did for a living, allegedly, didn't bother me. Granted, I learned, and before I knew it, I opened his garage one day and saw over thirty pounds of weed.

I, being a pothead, didn't complain as I only had 50/50 custody of my oldest daughter, Lucy. Therefore, I had more free time than needed as I didn't work either. Fifty percent of the time, I was with Marco, living it up, and the other 50% of the time, I was busy being the best mom I could be. Talk about double lives. While the parenting plan the courts devised was still in place, Lucy started to act strangely. I thought it was the transition of going back and forth from my house to her biological father's house or if he had a girlfriend or something. I had no idea what

I was up against. She started to function as if she had always done something wrong. She was constantly apologizing when she shouldn't be, hiding behind pillows when asked a simple question, and explaining that she couldn't tell me without me even asking a question. I just assumed it was her father's new girlfriend or, like I said, the transition. Lucy's behavior worsened after three months of me dating Marco and having three months of 50/50 custody. She was wetting the bed frequently, always crying, and screaming she couldn't tell me. Well, one day, she came home from her dad's crying. She was complaining about her "girly parts" hurting. I took a quick look, and it was bright red.

"Lucy, what happened?" I asked as I looked at her.

She replied sadly, "Daddy stuck something up there."

"Say what?" I yelled.

It was a mother's worst nightmare. I took a deep breath, grabbed my car keys, and rushed to the police station to write a statement.

As I walked out, Lucy tried to stop me. "Mommy, my dad is going to hurt me if I tell anyone." She cried.

"Baby, I'm not scared of your daddy, but he is about to be afraid of me." I replied.

Minutes later, I arrived at the police station, refusing to be that mother who didn't believe their kid. My mother stayed home with Lucy as she searched for one of the best family attorneys she could find. At the station I filled out a statement and chose to press charges. Lucy was only three then, and no three-year-old would make something like that up. I filled out four police statements, called DCF 3 times, and had her evaluated. I did everything that made sense. They claimed I was coaching her due to her age and the lack of proof. They ended up granting her father, Nick, the continued 50/50 custody. I lost my mind, as any good mother would. After that, I was prescribed heavy antidepressants and I tried to cope with the fact that there was nothing I could do to save my daughter from her "junkie" father who molested her. There was one option that I was contemplating, but it would leave my daughter without any parents. So, I prayed that there would be no more incidents and that, eventually, I would get full custody once her dad started to get in trouble for other things. I thought I had scared him enough for him to stop and leave her alone in that aspect. Marco was furious! He was more of a father to Lucy than her biological father ever was. He was there for me. Hugging him took my pain away momentarily, and I would take any relief that was available. We would just lay on the floor of his apartment, and I would cry while he held me and told me that everything would work itself out and that he would always be there for us. He wasn't lying. He stood by my side through thick and thin. He even paid for the attorney to help try and get full custody. I don't know what I would have done without him during this time.

After realizing that there was nothing I could do, besides keeping an eye on it, I had to let go because it was eating me alive. Her biological father was an alcoholic and a drug addict who was a threat to her and anyone he was around, which is why I left him in the first place. He lied to me for a couple of years about his habit before I left him, not knowing he was also a pedophile. One day while I was still living with Nick, Lucy was playing with her tiny basketball hoop, and when the ball hit the backboard, a "baggie" fell to the floor. Only two years old at the time, Lucy was still putting everything in her mouth. Luckily, I was there to grab and dispose of the bag before anything happened. Astonished, I waited until Nick left the house, (I am notorious for leaving without the men knowing) and had my mom and aunt meet me there to fill up their cars with my stuff. It took us hours to finish. I took everything that was able to fit in three vehicles. After we finally finished, we drove back to my mom's house. When we got there, we unloaded the cars and began to unpack. As we were unpacking, I kept getting phone calls from Nick, but I ignored him. As far as I was concerned, we were never married, so I had full custody of Lucy until a judge ordered differently. We unpacked and organized as I disregarded my phone and moved into my mom's beautiful house. It felt like a fresh beginning! Like I was free. That could also be because my mom had me quit my full-time job to focus on Lucy and myself. That woman is an angel. No matter the situation, she was my support system, and I will forever be grateful for her. Not soon after, I met Marco.

8

The End

Now, back to planning for a baby. I went to the OBGYN, got my IUD removed, and explained that we were trying to have a baby. I was so excited, and I would tell anyone who would listen! We tried but only had a 3-day time limit to make it happen. Unfortunately, it didn't work in that period, which was probably for the best. Marco still had a terrible temper, though it was not towards me or the children. If anything, his temper flared if you disrespected me or dared to disrespect our children. Other than that, he was very level-headed. However, neither one of us was thinking clearly as we decided our next move to have a threesome. It wasn't just any threesome. It was a threesome with Marco's best friend's wife, Rafa. Her husband had been beating her, and she recently found out he was cheating, so she wanted to get back at him by sleeping with us. We weren't complaining. We wanted to try something risky before having another baby and thought it would be fun, and it was alright. It could have been better, but it was alright, nonetheless. Being that it was my second threesome, I had high hopes it would be better than the first one, and it was. I don't regret any of it. Experimenting is normal and fun with a partner you trust and love. Once the night was over, Rafa left. Then she dared to complain to her mother about what happened and even went and told her husband, Jose, that she had just had a threesome with us. After all, it was her idea, and she knows that Jose is violent and has more than one gun. She didn't even give us a heads-up, and when she did, it was already too late. I remember trying to de-escalate the situation. I took the phone from Marco to talk to Rafa and calm her down before Marco lost his cool. While I was trying to calm Rafa down, Jose started talking shit to me in the background. All Marco heard was another man's voice yelling at me. Frankly, he was not okay with that. He took the phone and threatened Jose, and Marco wasn't the type to not follow through on his threats, allegedly.

Days later, I was getting phone calls from Rafa saying that her house had been shot up by my husband, allegedly. She then called the police and told them what she thought happened. Fortunately, her story changed more than once. However, once the police were alerted, they surrounded our house, and I mean, we were SURROUNDED. It was a SWAT team. Keep in mind they had no idea what was inside the safe in our house. They were only there for the alleged shooting. I walked outside to move my car, and I had 5 to 6 rifles pointed at me by SWAT team members. I quickly raised my hands, and Marco immediately came outside behind me. He also put his hands in the air and behind his head. The officers ordered him to walk slowly backward towards them until they apprehended him, getting his hands into zip ties, as handcuffs did not fit his wrists.

The SWAT team officers told me to go back inside the house, and I did not hesitate. I ran inside and made a few phone calls to see what I could do. Something had to be done as there was over $121,000 in cash, over four hundred grams of cocaine, eight guns, and 4.5 pounds of marijuana in the safe in the garage, allegedly. I was panicking beyond belief, and then I heard a knock at the door. The last thing I wanted to do was answer it, but I knew I had to. I opened the door, and a detective was standing there with three SWAT team officers behind him with rifles.

"Everyone has to leave the house while we search it," the detective commanded.

I replied. "No!"

"Why not? What do you mean?" He asked.

"You guys are scaring my children with these massive guns surrounding our home, pointing them at windows that my kids are looking out of," I explained.

"Well, ma'am, everyone has to leave the house immediately."

"Do y'all have a warrant?"

"No, not at the moment, but we need to search the house."

I sighed. "Buh bye," I replied and closed the door in their faces.

After that, I began to freak out again because I knew my time was limited as they prepared a warrant. An hour passed, and then I finally decided to leave the house with the kids.

When we made it outside, I asked the detective. "Why is my husband being detained? (not married yet but may as well have been)."

"He is involved in an alleged shooting, and we have reasons to believe that there is a fugitive in your house."

It was complete bullshit! The detective then showed me a video of a car driving away from the crime scene. They weren't able to capture a face or a license plate. I explained to the detective that it could have been anyone. They were disappointed they had no objective evidence against Marco other than what someone had told them. I walked down to the end of the street with the girls to our friend Russel's house. As the detective followed behind us, Russel let us in when we arrived. I called my mom to pick me and the kids up. After holding it together for as long as possible, I had a full-blown panic attack. My mother finally arrived not long after and picked us up. However, there was one last thing: the dogs.

The dogs were still in the house, and I knew they were waiting for the warrant as the street was still completely closed 6 hours later. When my mom arrived, I decided to give it a shot and ask the detective if I could go inside and get my dogs. It was a German Shepherd and a Chiweenie. Fortunately, he agreed, and I got them out and into my mom's car. After that, we got out of there. I spent most of the night calling Marco's friends and trying to raise money in advance for his attorney so they could be there at his first appearance. I did all this while the children slept peacefully in their rooms at my mom's house. Eventually, I raised the $10,000 for the attorney, who showed up at Marco's first court appearance. Thank goodness Marco was issued a bond. It was a substantial bond, and I had to raise money to pay for it. Anyhow, I did it!

I raised the money to bail him out by calling in several favors from our friends and family. The day when I was leaving to set the bond, DCF showed up at my house. What else could go wrong? I told them I had an emergency and scheduled to meet with them afterward. I went to get Marco out first, as a shift change at the facility where he was being held was about to happen soon, and I wanted to get him out before then. I got to the bail bonds office and put all the cash on the table. They gave me a look I'd never been given. It was one of shock and curiosity. They took the money, counted it, and posted the bail after my mom signed off on the paperwork.

After that, I called DCF to let them know I would be home. Trust me, you don't want to mess with those motherfuckers. They are above the law. They met me at my mom's house and asked us both to take a drug test. We declined because we both smoked weed. That didn't sit well with DCF.

One of them told me, "You need to find a family member who could pass a drug test, and then the children would be placed with them. If not, they would go into the foster system."

"Oh my God! Really?" My heart dropped into my stomach, and my chest hurt. I couldn't breathe.

Was this happening? Is this reality? I asked myself. My kids are my everything! I could not imagine life without them. But I had no choice as they would take them whether I liked it or not. I called my step-mother and my dad and told them to come get my kids, as they had officially been taken away from me.

Losing The Kids

I no longer had any control or custody of my children, nor did Marco. We immediately got an attorney and put a case plan in place. The plan included random drug tests every week, parenting classes, domestic violence classes, NA classes, and weekly check-ins with our case manager. It was overwhelming, and that's not including Marco's classes and needing a real job on top of it all. During the time my "dad" and "step-monster" had my children, they gave us the mandatory minimum amount of time with our kids and were not willing to supervise our visits. Therefore, we saw them 4 hours a week, in public areas, with an approved supervisor. Because that's not difficult enough, they told our case manager they no longer wanted Marco or me to be allowed on their property.

My so-called dad was making the situation as traumatic as possible. I don't care if he was just listening to his psychotic wife. It wasn't what I thought would happen when handing my children over to them. They could have let me stay at their house all day with the children to take care of them and be there for them, but instead, they made it the bare minimum of 4 hours a week with 2 Facetime calls a week. It was torture! Plus, COVID hit. The world turned upside down. People wore masks, we went on lockdown, and all visitations were canceled. For us, this meant not seeing our children, besides Facetime, for two and a half months.

Also, my birthday landed right in the middle of that phase. I woke up on my birthday morning with not only no children but to find out my grandmother, who raised me, had passed away. It was one of the worst days of my life. I got to FaceTime the kids, but that's it. I also had to miss my grandmother's ceremony due to my random drug tests. If I left the state and missed a drug test, it would be considered positive, and I couldn't take that chance. All it would take is one positive drug test for us to have to start from the beginning again. It was an unbearable day that I wasn't sure I would make it through, but I did. Crying the whole time, but I made it through, tears and all. I hated my dad and his wife. They did everything possible to ensure we wouldn't get our girls back. My "step-monster" would even write caregiver notes on why the children should not be allowed back in our custody. She wrote three long ones. However, you can't keep them from us if we don't mess up.

As my "step-monster," yes, that's her name, continued to try and keep us from our children. She would call my case manager and complain about anything she could think of. Although her complaints were utterly ridiculous, they were still complaints, nonetheless. My dad would chime in as well, talk about disappointment. Luckily, I got a level-headed case manager who wasn't blinded by my "step-monster's" hate for me. My case manager constantly had to stand up for me within the seven months we didn't have the children in our care. No matter how many times anyone asked, my dad and his wife could never produce an excuse as to why they suddenly hated us but wanted our children. I don't know how they did it, as my dad couldn't even raise me as a child. He left when I was one year old and returned when I was ten, but that is another story for another day. As time passed, Marco and I didn't miss a single class or drug test and passed all of them. We stayed steady with this for seven months, while everyone and their mother wanted to watch us fail. So, they say there is always a silver lining in every situation. Well, one had appeared in the parking lot in front of our condominium. It was a baby kitten, no more than two weeks old. I was ecstatic, as I still had a form of a baby with me. Something to give me purpose on a day-to-day basis. Something that needed me, but maybe not as much as I needed her. Walking up to the garage, I was worried Marco would disagree with keeping the kitten. His cute, big-hearted self welcomed this baby kitten with open arms. We named her Simba. She was a tiny calico tabby cat. Simba helped me cope with the loss of the kids.

Well, while we were following every rule and being on our best behavior, Lucy's father was charged with having possession of meth as well as child neglect of someone else's children. They had left three children in a trailer, unattended, for three days with no AC. The kids eventually locked themselves out of the trailer, looking for food or water.

The neighbors saw them and asked, "Do you have any adults with you in your house?"

They responded, "No, they haven't been home in 3 days, and we are hungry".

The neighbor then called the police to get the situation figured out. As the police were about to leave, Lucy's father pulled up in a truck with three other adults. The police report stated that he had a naked 11-month-old baby in the back seat of his car with no car seat. He went to jail, so I didn't have to worry about him sabotaging our case plan like my stepmom, dad, and his parents would stop at nothing to do.

I had never felt this type of pain in my life. I would go to bed crying, missing Lexi, who used to sleep between us every night—waking up to Lexi not being there with her arm around my neck like I would wake up every morning. Whatever the case, I could not stop crying and sobbing over losing my children. Marco was more than supportive, knowing he fucked up. He would hold me for what felt like hours while I cried. He didn't leave my side. He wouldn't even let me shower alone to make sure I was okay. We started going to the gym together when we didn't have classes and before they shut down because of Covid. It was an excellent outlet for me; it helped my hunger, it helped my anger, and it helped my depression. I would work out with Marco until I couldn't breathe anymore, until there was some relief to the pain, I felt every day. Sober, no antidepressants, no weed, no anything. I was completely and utterly sober. Which in most cases would be a great thing. However, I should have been on antidepressants. I was in such a horrible place, and some people may call it cheating, but hell, I would cheat if it meant not feeling that pain and rejection constantly. But I didn't "cheat" and take antidepressants, which almost ruined my marriage. I suffered from severe PTSD, anxiety, and chronic depression. I pulled myself together, got through my mood swings, and learned to control myself as well as Marco. Maybe not with as much grace as I would like, but I got through it.

About five months before getting the kids back, my father started allowing us to see Lexi more, as Lucy lived with her grandparents and did not want much to do with me. Being older, she held more of a grudge as she understood what was going on, and I honestly can't blame her. The people she was around were toxic, constantly talking poorly about Marco and me, which didn't help us. When we had our two hours, we would take the kids to the pool or the playground to spend time with them. It had to be somewhere public. We celebrated Lucy's birthday at a playground and made the best of it as we relied on my mother financially for many things. Not being able to afford things was something Marco and I were not used to but got used to. Eventually, we got an eviction letter and decided to rent out our condo (allegedly) while we could and move into my mother's house. It worked out great. They didn't evict him for a few months, so that money helped.

My mom had sold the huge house she owned with her sister Martha, a big bitch, but always there for us when we needed her, and rented another big house in the same neighborhood for her and my family. It was beautiful, with a fenced-in backyard, a heart-shaped pool and spa, four bedrooms, three living rooms, and more. It was perfect, and both kids got their room. The dogs loved the backyard; we loved the pool, and the neighborhood itself was a fantastic community in general. That must explain why the homeowner's association fees were so high. They would throw small fairs for every holiday and have Santa come through on his sled during nights in December. It was a dream house in a dream neighborhood. Marco and I moved in as soon as the lease was established. Not only that, but it was only 15 minutes from where the girls were living. In the middle of everything, a grade-A school was built in the neighborhood only for the children that lived there. Everything was falling in our favor, and my dad caught wind of it. We were getting the kids back. They could do nothing about it. We never failed a drug test or missed one or a class or a call with our case manager. Marco now had a tax-paying job to provide for the children, and we had a beautiful home to raise them in. There was no denying we deserved to have our children back, and my dad knew if he ever wanted to see the kids again, he would have to get back on my side.

We had earned unsupervised visitation with the children, and my father began dropping Lexi off and letting her spend the day at my house. Once I saw all these little changes he was making, like becoming more of a father figure and grandpa and trying to become more involved. I wanted to give him another chance as he was trying to change. Marco and my mother disagreed with me and thought he wasn't being genuine. I didn't listen to them and pursued a relationship with my dad, a real relationship, for the first time. Now, I just had to get Marco and my mom on board so that we could all be civil, at the least. Hopefully, he could prove himself over time, but only time will tell. More time passed, and as I kept letting my dad into my life, so did Marco and Mom. The seven-month marking period as to the earliest we could get our kids back was right around the corner, and then the day had come.

The court date determining if we got custody back was here. I was less nervous because it was a Zoom meeting due to COVID-19. Lucy's grandpa chimed in and asked for full custody of Lucy in the middle of the court hearing. The judge asked him if he wanted Lucy to go to a foster home because she was not allowed at their house unsupervised due to Lucy's father's recent arrest. I was sweating during the court hearing, but we got the news we had been waiting and working towards since we lost them. The judge granted us custody back!

Not only that, but the judge also granted me full custody of Lucy because of her father's recent arrest. That day, we got to pick up our kids from that evil "step-monster's" house. We gathered all their stuff and packed up the truck. My step-monster was now being nice to me, knowing that was the only way she could see the kids again. See, I'm a firm believer that if you are toxic in my relationship with me, you are also harmful to my kids. I'm also a firm believer in "Fuck You". Therefore, she wouldn't see my kids because it's not good for anyone's mental health. But that's just my opinion.

We had already had the girl's bedrooms ready to go and a welcome home cake on the table for when they arrived. Words cannot explain mourning what is alive while fighting to bring it back to you. My heart was so whole! I couldn't wait to show the kids their rooms and unpack and organize all their stuff! We unloaded all the things we sent them with and some additional older ripped clothes from my "step-monster" that I quickly threw away. It felt like a dream I never wanted to wake up from. My babies were home right where they belonged. With me, my mom, and Marco all under one roof, it made me beyond happy, grateful, and extremely humble. It took a catastrophe to realize I was not above anyone, especially the government. They could do whatever they wanted when they wanted. They continued to do weekly virtual phone calls and in-person therapy sessions for the next four months after they returned home, which didn't bother me at all as I had nothing to hide and was going to be the best mom I could be.

Not only did this experience humble me, but it also made me a better mother. As the saying goes, you don't know what you have until it's gone. When you lose something that important, it changes you. It makes you want to be better. Thinking back on times, I could have handled things differently. I could have cuddled them more and given them more kisses. Showing them how much I love them. So, at the end of all this, getting my children back, I no longer went to sleep with any regrets of the day regarding the kids. I used to go to sleep going over everything I should have done differently and finding myself wanting to wake up my kids and hug them. I no longer had these thoughts before bed. I went to bed in peace, knowing I appreciated my children more than anything, and finally had them back.

Once the children were home, Lucy still wasn't happy with me or Marco. She was sassy and very distant. It took her around four months to start trusting us again. Honestly, I cannot blame her. I cannot imagine how everything impacted her life. She would defy me in the meanest ways and throw fits, and I finally had enough. I never put my hands on my kids, but I WILL take away their favorite things, including the Wi-Fi. Once that power struggle was settled, I was in control again, and Lucy was back to her usual sweet, funny, and clever self.

Lexi wasn't as affected by anything as she was when she was young. They tried to brainwash her, just like they did to Lucy. It only didn't work with Lexi. She was too young to understand what was happening. She was so happy to be back with her family that she didn't think twice. My "step-monster" and dad divorced a couple of months before we got the kids back, so my dad tried to be a part of our family. Not only did my step-monster not want him at the house anymore, but he also would have never seen the girls again, and he knew it. Let's just say he messed up a lot. So, he weaseled back into my life like the roach he was. He never got over my mom, 32 years later, and is still in love with her. It had nothing to do with me. More time passed, and my mom and

Marco started accepting my dad into the family. It was great for us. I've never witnessed my mom and dad getting along.

10

The So Called "Father"

After about a year, they got a little too close. Don't get me wrong, I wanted them to be friends, but my dad had been married five times already, and there was no way I would trust him with my mom. I'm the only person I trust to have good intentions for my mother. I'm a mommy's girl to the fullest, and no one would ever hurt her if I could stop it. My mom wanted to go to West Virginia, and my dad immediately volunteered to drive her there, which was a surprise. The man can't co-sign on a car for me with his 700-credit score, but he would do anything for my mom. I didn't understand it at all. What did I do wrong to make him have no emotional attachment towards me? All this made me think and resent my dad, especially when he was with my mom in West Virginia. Little did I know, Marco had felt the same way as I did, resentful. He wanted to solve the issue and talk to my dad when he got back from West Virginia, and he told my dad that over the phone. At the same time, my dad was trying to move into the garage of our house. Neither Marco nor I were happy with this new idea, but my dad kept pressing it, and my mom allowed it. We didn't argue with her because my mom paid all the bills.

As soon as my mom and dad returned from West Virginia, Marco asked my dad to talk to him privately, and my dad threw his hand in his face and said, "Not now."

For those of you who don't know Marco like I do, he's not someone you disrespect and get away with. Marco immediately began yelling at my dad, calling him names. "You're a bitch, you kept our kids from us, and now you want to live with us?"

You would think this upset me, given that he's my father, but I enjoyed seeing my dad getting what he deserved. Call me twisted, but I never had an emotional attachment with my father since I didn't spend time together with him until I was ten, and even then, he barely came around. Until my "step-monster" (his fifth wife) came along, he was only nice to me when it was convenient for him. Henceforth, I had no emotion towards the terrifying Marco yelling at him. Eventually, they took it outside, and I just watched quietly from behind the gate. I knew this was a "my monkeys," "my circus" deal, but I still didn't care. As I watched through the gate in the backyard, my mom stood between Marco and my dad. My dad looked scared.

Then, out of nowhere, Marco spits over my mom's head, and it lands right on my dad's face! I was shocked but surprisingly satisfied. I had many years to wish I were the one to spit in his face. After seeing this, I walked around the gate and got Marco, my mom, and my dad in his brand-new truck. Marco grabbed the door handle, but he took off. My mom was freaking out on Marco for everything, but little did she know I was about to jump in on Marco's behalf. My mother didn't understand what had just happened, as she missed the events leading up to it. She was starting to have feelings for my so-called dad again, and I couldn't have that. So, I intervened and put everything out on the table. Everything that bothered me, why he was the wrong person to be around, his toxicity. Eventually, my mom, Marco, and I worked it all out, and we cut all communication with my dad, as this wasn't the first incident, just the first one since Marco had been around. As families do, we all overcame it and went about our lives. However, my mom was still speaking to my dad, so I went through her phone while she was sleeping, like some creepy boyfriend. But I had to know because my dad is money-hungry and still trying to move into our garage. I was right. She was still talking to him on the phone and texting him. It was so out of character for my mom since she only dated one person since my dad left us. And it made me angry because the majority, well, all the time, my mom was mine and only mine, even when she had a boyfriend. So, of course, I took these texts very seriously and confronted her the next day.

She said, "I enjoy talking to him. I don't see the harm in a few text messages."

I was infuriated. I could have had smoke coming out of my ears. Did I hear that right? I reminded her why we didn't like him and that we should not be in that situation again. Of course, my mom eventually took my side and stopped talking to my dad after several hiccups.

These included my so-called father texting me vulgar things such as, "You're a spitting image of my mother, and she was a piece of shit" (who was an alcoholic who stabbed her boyfriend three times).

He would also say things like, "Look for me in the courtroom, I'll be there!" and "Peace out bitch, see you on the other side." It was enough for my mom to cut him off completely, but not before yelling at him.

I knew the time would come when my "step-monster" would contact me, wanting to see the kids again. Best moment ever! No way was I letting my children around her and her toxic mentality. No, thank you! I didn't even respond.

I I

The "Father," Nick

Lucy had a different father than Lexi. His name is Nick. He is a troubled alcoholic who eventually grew into an avid drug user, and I don't mean the petty stuff. He was smoking meth and heroin, eventually shooting it up. However, it was only the drinking habit that I knew of when we met and started dating. He also had a best friend named Russ. Russ was a good guy and a fantastic chef. Unfortunately, he drank with Nick and worked with him. Nick owned a pool business, which he barely attended to. At first, I didn't think the drinking was that bad, even though I'm not a drinker myself. I prefer to smoke.

Anyway, let's start from the beginning. My mom and Aunt had just bought an enormous house with a pool and screened-in deck. It was in a beautiful neighborhood close to Disney World, filled with forests and beautiful nature trails. This is the house that I spoke about earlier, where we brought Lexi home. Coincidentally, my mother had hired a pool service company, which happened to be Nick's company. Before Nick was into hard-core drugs, he just drank a lot. But drinking hadn't affected his looks yet, and I was attracted to him. When I was by the pool one day, he asked me how old I was. I told him I was 19 years old, and he told me he was twenty-two and wanted to take me out on a date.

I agreed to this date and was honestly excited. Looking back, yuck! But you wanted to know my story.

We hit it off on our first date and began to see each other quite often. We had been together for about two and a half years when I had finally saved up enough money for my boob job. Unlike some lucky women, I was not blessed in that department, so I took matters into my own hands. I had a steady 9 am to 6 pm Monday through Friday job, which is how I was able to save up enough money to get my breast implants. I remember I paid the price in full, got all my pre-blood work done, and then, it was time to go under the knife. Before the surgery, the staff is required to do a mandatory pregnancy test. Surprisingly, I tested positive. I told them it must be a false positive and to do it again. They did, and it was positive again. I was so upset that I began to cry and stomp my feet like a child. I went in for a boob job and left with a baby. Of course, it was the biggest blessing of my life, but damn the timing sucked. Not only that, but I had just turned twenty-one, and Nick and I's relationship had been on the rocks. I was planning to leave him after my surgery, which made things a bit sticky for me. I decided I was keeping this beautiful blessing whether he liked it or not. He didn't. He would tell me he didn't sign up for this whenever I had a craving, a mood swing, or a contraction. In the beginning, he wanted me to have an abortion, but I was working my ass off and had no intention of any abortion.

Eventually, we saved enough money to move out of Nick's parents' house. His parents found us a great condominium close to their house and my mom's. It was the perfect little three-bedroom townhome to start a family in. Nick's parents put down a sizeable down payment for us, which made our mortgage manageable for my income. I also contributed all the money I had saved to get my breast implants, but I did not want my name on the lease. Something told me not to, that if I needed out, I needed to get out with a clean slate and not worry about the house getting destroyed. So, the house was in Nick's name only. We couldn't move in immediately, so we stayed at my mom's house for two weeks when Lucy was born. Thanks to both sides of my grandparents, I had a huge bedroom and everything we needed for the baby. We stayed at my mom's house for the first two weeks, and it was the only time Nick was hands-on with Lucy. It is because I had a scheduled C-section due to my lack of hips. They were too small, and I was at risk of breaking my tailbone and my pelvic bone, so the doctor suggested that this would be the best option for me and my baby.

We were then in our new home as a "family." We bought furniture, a TV, and everything we needed to be comfortable. Well, I bought it with my credit. It was at that point that things got real. Nick's parents no longer supervised him. I found out he was twenty-seven when he met me at 19 years old, and we had a newborn baby to take care of now. Well, for me to take care of. I wasn't even working 40 to 60 hours weekly anymore. Nick's parents watched the baby while I was at work, busting my ass to make ends meet to pay our bills.

The circumstances put a considerable strain on our relationship and made me not want to be around Nick at any time. I paid the bills and cared for the baby while he drank beer with Russ. Financially, I was struggling. My weight was down to ninety-six pounds, and Nick acted differently, almost paranoid. Then, he started staying up for days at a time. It only progressed over a more extended amount of time. He would max out on day five, then sleep for two days. After that, he would wake up and do it all over again. Being as naive as I was then, I knew something was up. But I didn't know what. Who goes that long without sleeping? His behavior began to spin out of control like no one was home. It was someone else I didn't know or know what they could be capable of. This type of psychosis episode would occur about every other month, and I was at the brunt end of it, as usual. Luckily, I have tough skin because that was not easy. I slept without clothes on, only my bra and underwear, and he would wake me up around 4 am when these episodes happened. He would wake me by pulling the covers off me and telling me to get off his bed because it was "his" mattress, meaning it was from his parents' house. The first time this happened, I was terrified.

I didn't know how to handle the situation as he was unpredictable and out of his mind. Being that it was the first time it had happened, I chose to get angry. I got mad and began yelling at Nick and telling him to start paying bills before he told me to get out of bed. He retaliated and just laid into me. All my insecurities were brought to light. I went from angry to scared. I thought I was handling this wrong and decided to do what he asked until I could leave the house to get to work. I went downstairs with my blanket and lay on the couch, as I had to be up for work in about 2 hours. He followed me down the stairs and continued to tell me we were over and to sign some non-existent paperwork about Lucy. He went on and on, so I got up and went outside to smoke a cigarette because now I'm irritated, tired, and worried about my well-being all at the same time. I get out and sit down. Two seconds later, here comes Nick talking more shit. I stopped listening to him because he wasn't making sense, and I didn't want to endanger myself. So, I did what I always do: call his parents. I called his father (who is just incredible in so many ways) and told him what was going on because Nick would not let me leave the house. Whenever I tried to leave the house, he would block my exit and not let me through. Mind you, I had Lucy with me because I was NOT going to leave her with him, not that I would any other day. I dropped Lucy off every morning before work at Nick's parent's house. They got to raise her for the first two or three years of her life due to my work schedule and working overtime to make ends meet. Once the bills were paid, there was nothing left for food. My mother occasionally came over with a trunk full of food for the house, but I never got to eat any of it. Nick would stay up all night and eat everything in the fridge.

After about eight months of living together and being financially in control, we struggled. Conveniently, Nick's younger sister Sarah, my age, needed a place to live because she didn't want to live with her parents anymore. Keep in mind we were the same age. Since I struggled to put food on the table, I agreed to let her move into our guest bedroom upstairs if she helped with our mortgage—a big mistake. I'd rather starve knowing what I know now. She was just as bad as Nick, staying up all night (not five days in a row, but enough), falling asleep in Lucy's princess tent, stacking the beer cans a foot above the trash can, waking up and cracking open a beer. Then, one day, she came home from work sober (or so I thought), and when she walked in, she asked if she could spend time together with Lucy in her room. Since I was there, if anything happened, I agreed to let her take Lucy upstairs to her room. After about 15 minutes, I hear a BOOM coming from upstairs. I immediately ran upstairs, praying Lucy was okay. I run into Sarah's room and see Lucy (my one-year-old) sitting in a pot of bong water in her diaper. I took her diaper off and noticed a 20-pound mirror knocked over. I looked over, and Sarah passed out drunk, so I took the whole pot of bong water and tossed it on her face. Talk about a rude awakening, a furious mom, and bong water in your eyes and mouth. She didn't do anything but start spitting. It is safe to say Sarah and I never really got along; we were two completely different people. Also, I didn't intentionally do things Sarah enjoyed, like drinking. I would never drink with them because I didn't want to encourage or give them a reason to justify their drinking addiction.

Things continued to spiral downward with Sarah, Nick, and me. Their behavior continued to get worse while I was busting my ass at work and taking care of baby Lucy. They just got in my way of a normal lifestyle, which started to build up emotionally, and I kept it inside. Other than vacuuming at 7 am and hitting her door with it, that was about as petty as I went. Sarah began bringing men I didn't know into the house and letting them stay the night. It was a different guy every week I had never seen before. Her room was directly next to Lucy's, which made me nervous for obvious reasons. So, whenever Sarah would bring a guy home, I would grab Lucy and bring her to my room to make sure nothing happened to her, being that I knew nothing about them. As these events continued, I began to grow angrier and more resentful. There were better ways to handle the situation. Six months down the road, things hit rock bottom at the house. It was me against the Pulleys. Sarah and Nick just saw me as a party pooper who worked too much and took things too seriously. Well, one night after work, I had plans to have two of my best guy friends over to meet Nick and see Lucy. It is the same night that Sarah invites all nine of her new co-workers to our condo. Seriously?!

She entered the door with two Jack Daniels handles and was ready to drink. Once I saw this, I knew the entire night had just taken a turn for the worse. I had nine strange men in my house while my 1-year-old daughter slept upstairs. I was infuriated. She made these plans without telling us and knew I was having my two friends over to meet Nick. Now that I had nine strange, drunk men in my house, I stopped smoking and sobered up. I knew tonight wasn't going to end well. I had it. I was done, over it. As I watched this whole "party" go on in my house, one of Sarah's friends got extremely drunk and started acting bazaar. By bazaar, I mean standing in the open front doorway, leaning back and forth and not responding to anyone, just standing there, back, and forth. Nick took it upon himself to move the guy and punch him in the face to "knock it out of him." Being the guys they were, my friends immediately jumped in as these kids' friends began to come after Nick.

Before I knew it, it was a complete brawl, and I could barely distinguish who was fighting whom except Nick. He was standing there watching all this happen after he started the entire thing. I look to the other side of me, and Sarah is beating up MY friend who wouldn't hit a girl back. I immediately ran and tapped Sarah on the shoulder. She turned to look at me, and I punched her in the throat. Boy, did that feel good! I've wanted to get my hands on Sarah for a long time. I then went to help my friend, and he said my name. I looked behind me, and Sarah punched me in the forehead.

I said, "SARAH!"

She then screamed, "JESSIE!"

I got my friend up, and everyone went inside, fearing the cops would get called. Once in the house with everyone who had just fought, I decided I wasn't done with Sarah. I chased her up the stairs, plowing through the baby gate to get to her. I stopped because breaking the baby gate made me realize what I was doing. Eventually, Sarah returned to the kitchen, and her brother Nick stood beside her. I began walking back and forth, side to side of the kitchen, slowly getting closer to her, keeping eye contact the whole time. I was furious. All those months of her driving me insane have led to this moment. I continued getting closer to Sarah and eventually made it up to her face-to-face. She was leaning against the top cabinets, with the microwave (attached to the top of the cabinets) to her right.

As I stood face to face with Sarah and had her backed up against the kitchen cabinets, she said, "What are you going to do?"

Because what am I going to do? I wouldn't say I like being called out. If I am, I respond. So, I reacted. I threw the best right hook of my life, and the back of her head hit the kitchen cabinets. Then I grabbed her by the top of the hair, threw her on the floor, and continued to swing. Let me remind you, I was one hundred pounds and 5 9'. Sarah was 160 pounds and 5'9 as well. It wasn't an unfair fight, well, for me (keep in mind that I had just had surgery. I got my breast implants done four days prior). I kept swinging until someone pulled me off her. I then left with my two friends and went to their house till things settled down. Worried about Lucy being there, I called Nick's dad to get her as they lived down the street. As I sit at my friend's house, I get a text from Sarah about a statement she wrote for the police about the fight. She was trying to press charges. Nice try, Sarah! She was on probation for a DUI she had gotten that year, and I had overheard her probation officer's name a few times. Lucky me.

I responded that if she pressed charges on me, that was fine, but I would press them back, and it being my first charge, I would get a slap on the wrist and probation at most. On the other hand, Sarah was not a first-time offender and wouldn't be treated like one. I quickly reminded her of this, and she decided against pressing charges. Now, there was the issue of where she was going to live. After she brought out the side in me, I refused to go back with Lucy, and we stayed at my mom's house until we could figure out our living situation. Well, Sarah had decided to leave the state entirely that same week. She moved to Colorado to start over. I moved back in once she was all moved out and, on her way, out of the state.

12

Newish Begining

Once I moved back in, things got worse between Nick and me. He resented me for Sarah moving to Colorado. They were close and had all the same bad habits that strengthened their bond. Call it a trauma bond. Anyhow, he began to use more, and the psychosis got even worse. Around 4 am (again) one night, he ripped the covers off me, and I had to escape and drive to my mom's house in my bra and some shorts that I was able to throw on quickly. I got ready for work that morning, and my mom watched Lucy for me. Later that week, I got home one day after picking up Lucy, and Nick was not home.

We had a little basketball hoop on our front door for Lucy to play with. She threw her tiny basketball, and it hit the backboard. The hit of the ball made a small baggie filled with white stuff fall to the floor. Lucy was almost two and still putting everything in her mouth. She didn't get a hold of it because I was paying attention enough and got rid of it immediately. I decided that was the day I would leave him. After I flushed the baggie, I called my mom and explained to her the situation. I told her I needed to get out as soon as possible, and if she could take the next day off, he would not be home. I knew that the next day, he had his "pool route" he did once a week. That was my chance to get out without a fight. When he left that afternoon, my mom and aunt pulled up to start filling their cars with Lucy's and my stuff. We loaded my car, my mom's car, and my aunt's car with everything we could stuff in there. I left the house key and garage opener on the kitchen counter and went with Lucy and all my stuff.

The fact that Nick and I never got married meant I had sole custody of Lucy until I was taken to court. So, I held on to Lucy as long as I could until his parents paid for an attorney for him. I got served paperwork on Valentine's Day that I was being taken to court for custody of her. I had plans to go out with my rich boyfriend, Frank. He would spoil me and had a massive 12,000 sq ft house on Lake Butler. He was upset that I got this information the day he planned to go out for Valentine's Day. I canceled all my plans and began calling attorneys. Frank was not okay with this. He thought it could be handled later.

Let's say it didn't work out. Not only did Frank not help me pay for my attorney for Lucy (I'm a brat, I know), but he had me drugged at a museum. He took me out with his Chemist friend and his girlfriend. They seemed nice enough. We had a limousine for the night, and I was excited to go out and see the art displayed. I had never been to a museum before. The Chemist was the person making my drinks of ninety-nine bananas. I had only two drinks, and I blacked out the rest of the night. I woke up on the side of the road with people waking me up, and they were nice enough to let me use their phone to call my mom. I called my mom, and she immediately came to get me. That is what ended our relationship. Now, back to Valentine's Day.

I searched for attorneys and finally found one. It is expensive but worth it, given the circumstances. After a relentless, brutal fight in the courtroom, I knew he was a drug addict who could not care for Lucy safely. I fought until I had nothing left in me. Unfortunately, he ended up getting 50/50 custody, and there was nothing I could do to change the parenting plan until she was in school. I dealt with this and tried to be the best mom I could be when she was in my care, and I kept myself busy when she wasn't, to try and take my mind off it. Now, this is when I met Marco. Marco, being the man he was, paid for Lucy's attorney whenever a payment was needed. As time passed, Marco became more of a father to Lucy than Nick ever was. Marco had been paying for every birthday since she was three years old, buying her presents, being present, and loving her like his own. All of this was before Lexi.

13

Picking Up Where We Left Off

After a while, Lucy wanted to see her father. I was very hesitant, being that Nick was still addicted to meth and heroin. Lucy begged, so I eventually gave in, under one condition: his parents would supervise it. I thought that was reasonable considering the situation. His parents and I grew remarkably close after we got the kids back. I was unhappy with their behavior during the custody trial, but I forgave them because Lucy wanted me to. Once we got over that hurdle, we ended up bonding and having a great relationship where we would all hang out. They got to see Lucy whenever they wanted.

Lucy's paternal grandpa was like the father I never had. He always took care of me and prayed for me. He often told me that he was no angel when he was my age, so he understood what I was going through. I trusted them entirely, knowing Lucy would be okay in their care. I also had a feeling Nick wouldn't show up anyway, given his "disease." I was right. He visited her at his parent's house once or twice. It devastated Lucy, and that was just the beginning. He was not showing up when he said he would, missing birthdays and holidays, and not answering her phone calls. Yet, he was sending her bizarre text messages stating that I was in love with him, and that is why he didn't come around, how it was all my fault. He brought up my charges, and everything else. Luckily, Lucy was old enough to realize who was there for her and who wasn't. He had put her in danger, neglected, and ignored her. Lucy had enough of it. Once upon a time, he made her go door to door in his parents' neighborhood to sell Chex Mix and told Lucy the money was going towards a puppy he would buy her. However, he had ulterior motives. Lucy had to deal with this behavior from her dad while she was growing up. Somehow, it made her grow up much faster. She was able to see him until I received full custody after finishing my case plan. I didn't just get Lucy back. I took her back permanently. The reasons were undeniable. Lucy was not safe in her father's care. During our case plan, Nick got caught riding his bike in the middle of the night, wearing a backpack.

A police officer drove up and asked. "Where are you going?"

"A friend's house," Nick replied.

The officer stopped him and searched his bag and found meth with needles and some counterfeit money. Nick was arrested, but his parents posted his bail quickly, thinking I wouldn't find out about the incident. Between me and my mother, I checked the Orange County Clerk of Courts multiple times weekly. Therefore, we found out the next day after it happened. I immediately called my case manager and told her what his charges were and how the drug he was abusing was one you can't just quit but should seek medical rehab to ensure a clean recovery. She agreed but told him that if he passed four random drug tests, he could continue to have partial custody of Lucy.

Nick decided not to participate in this and lost all custody and rights to Lucy. To me, it was a blessing, but it was a curse to Lucy. She knew he had had a problem and resented him for it. The resentment turned into anger. I understood, not that my dad did half of the things Nick did, but I understood the anger of abandonment. I just tried to be there as much as I could for Lucy. Her father had done so much damage emotionally that she had barely any self-esteem left. He also texted her a recent picture of himself, and he looked like he was in his sixties. He quickly deleted it, but not before Lucy took a screenshot. She sent it to everyone. I don't blame her. He looked awful, and he knew it. Not only that, but in his mug shots that she also has access to, he has sores all over his face, and his mouth is twisted to the side. There was no denying it to Lucy. I would have if I could have sheltered her from this, but she was right there in the crossfire.

14

The Kids Are Home

Going from having no kids for seven months to having both back at the same time was overwhelming, I'm not going to lie. I made it more complicated than needed, as I had something to prove to my kids and everyone else watching me, waiting for me to make a mistake to hold against me as my case plan was still open. So yes, we had the kids back, but we were still taking our classes, and our case plan was still in place. This meant house calls, video calls, class completion, and random drug screenings. It was a lot to juggle with two kids, but I couldn't be happier or prouder of myself and Marco for how far we came. We had accomplished so much and got our kids back before our case plan ended, despite the odds stacked against us. We did it! Unfortunately, Marco still had an open case. It had been over a year, and they continued to push the trial date back further. I was not complaining. I cherished every moment I spent with him, as I knew it was limited. Was this his last Halloween? Last Christmas? It was the unknown that made everything that much more difficult. We spent as much time together as possible, even with him working 40 hours a week with an hour's commute. We made the best of it. On paper, he had a real, tax-paying job to show our case manager and the courts that he had changed his ways. We had changed our lifestyle entirely for the better, and it felt great.

Marco got into a horrible car accident five days before Christmas of 2020. From the car's look, it was unimaginable that he was still alive. After he was discharged from the hospital, we brought him home so he could settle. Luckily, he had no significant injuries and was in good health. What had happened was Marco was driving to a friend's house, and he had back issues, which caused him to be always cracking his neck. As he was cracking his neck, he must have broken a nerve that made him pass out at the wheel on the highway, going sixty-five mph. When he passed out, the car went over the guard rail, and the little vehicle flipped three times. Marco walked away without a stitch. Sometimes, I swear this man has a guardian angel. Thank God he was okay, but since the car was totaled, we were out of a vehicle when it was all said and done.

I was worried about how I would take the kids to school. School attendance for them was still essential in our case plan. I couldn't use Marco's car because, due to our case plan, one of us had to have a job, and he couldn't afford to lose it. The only plan that would work was to take my mom to work in the morning before taking the kids to school. It was painful, but it worked until I was able to figure something else out. Well, it took about six months to figure out how to afford a new car. After watching me struggle, Lucy's grandpa eventually bought me a used SUV. I couldn't have been more thrilled, as I had been asking my dad to co-sign a vehicle for me since the accident happened, and he refused. What a dad! He purchased three cars back-to-back and ruined his credit for himself. Luckily, Lucy's grandpa was a great father figure to me at this point in my life.

Now, having a car, I can provide for my family and be around my family. Given my schedule with the girls, I needed to figure out where to apply, so I tried Lucy's daycare. It would be a pleasant experience, given I had worked with children previously and loved it. Once I applied, I quickly found out I got the job. Not only did I get the job, but I also got to be an embers teacher. How exciting! I love my new job. The hours perfectly fit the girl's school schedule. However, being an embers teacher conflicted with my teaching in the classroom. Lucy would act out and expect special attention because her mother was her teacher. Eventually, I got moved to the adjoining classroom next to Lucy's. Her new teacher was another mom. Her daughter attended the daycare and was about three years old. She seemed nice enough, always chit-chatting with me. One day, that chit-chat turned into a serious conversation, at least for me.

She started explaining, "I have an abscessed tooth, and I am taking painkillers to be at work right now." She continued. "I'm not talking about the over-the-counter kind of stuff."

I was just listening as she spoke and told me everything. Why do people do this to me? I don't know. She told me, "I went to the hospital last night to make sure I had enough painkillers for today."

The next day at school, during lunch break, I was urged to tell my supervisor what I had heard. After all, the woman was taking care of and responsible for thirteen three-year-olds. It seemed unsafe for her to be on narcotics while caring for children. I told my supervisor. Remember that we were very short-staffed, and the company was nervous about losing more teachers, given the teacher-to-child ratio. She overlooked my concern and continued to let this teacher work under the influence, not to mention she was my daughter's teacher. I had to request my boss mainly because we have now finished our case plan! I no longer needed a job nor did I have to put up with this nonsense. Not only was she getting high while watching children, but she was also encouraging her almost 3-year-old daughter to play telephone using curse words. I was appalled as she laughed away, thinking it was hilarious.

On top of everything else, I wouldn't say I liked how they ran their company or the people employed there. I had to watch the baby room one day, and the usual preschool teacher explained how to get the children to take their naps. I'm thinking of a rocking chair, food, and bottles beforehand. You know, an excellent way to get a baby to sleep, considering there were only four children. She explained to me that she kicked the babies to get them to go back to sleep. It's not hard, but it's enough to make me uncomfortable. I went to my manager about the incident, and once again, she wrote it off and didn't take any measurements as to the repercussions of her actions. I went from a request to outright quitting. I could not be a part of an establishment that treated children that way. Even though it ended up with me no longer having a job, I felt at ease knowing my daughter was not attending that daycare anymore. I've heard horror stories, and they are very much accurate.

I was depressed over no longer being able to work at the same daycare as my daughter Lexi, and not to mention the lack of money. After about two months, I got off my ass and began filling out job applications at schools, as I didn't want to be subjected to daycare again. After applying to a few places, my favorite school hired me. I was beyond myself. See, my husband was working full time for a great company that also provided the kids and myself health insurance and provided for us financially. He loved his job and never missed a day. It was huge for our family after the lifestyle he allegedly lived, and I wanted to have the same impact. Granted, I didn't have to work; my mom is very well off and has no issue taking care of my family, but it's the principal. I wanted to help support and provide for my family as well. So, I did. I started working immediately as I was already qualified for the job and had all the certificates needed to begin. It was incredible; I got a 75% discount on their tuition. It made it easy for me on my salary as a VPK teacher to have them enrolled. It was a private Elementary school, and beautiful at that. The staff was friendly, I loved the other teachers, the children were great, and my kids got an excellent education and experience. We were all delighted even though we knew Marco was still on bond and had no idea what to expect. No matter how glad I was, I still had this hanging over my head.

15

⚯

Jail

Marco was eventually offered seven years for the alleged crime, but he turned it down and said he wanted to go to trial. Keep in mind that Marco was also NO snitch. When pressed, he refused to give any information, which did not help his case but left him with a 7-year plea deal. I was working happily at my private Elementary school for about five months, getting praised, being a favorite, helping the problem children, building relationships with these tiny humans, meeting all my kids' friends, and knowing if they were respectful students. However, it was all suddenly taken from me.

It was "Casual Friday," when you didn't have to wear uniforms and got to dress however you wanted (within reason, of course). Well, I chose to wear a bright pink shirt, jeans, cute white sneakers, and pink eye shadow that Friday. I was already ready for the weekend. There were some good upcoming fights that weekend, and I was eager to watch them. That morning, I got to work, opened my car door, and jumped out excitedly. When I turned around, I had four rifles pointed at me. Shit! There was a SWAT team surrounding me and my children, who were still in the car. This unfolded directly in front of the Elementary

71

school. I immediately threw my Apple watch in the car and closed the door. They then told me they had a phone and an arrest warrant.

I asked them if I could calm my children down. Once they realized that I was harmless, they allowed it. Honestly, I was ducking and dodging because parents and children I knew from the school were walking by, staring. What a remarkable impression! An entire SWAT team, in unmarked cars, for little old me. This was two years after Marco's arrest. I was just a VPK teacher! The officers told me I needed someone to pick up the kids, so I called both sides of the grandparents, and they came and got the children. Once my daughters left, the officers pulled me to the car of the detective who was on our case and sat me in the passenger seat.

I was quiet and livid as the detective sat on the driver's side. I would have turned myself in to avoid all that embarrassment and trauma on my children. I looked in the cup holder only to see a tape recorder with a red light on. I'm not stupid. Considering my mood, he would record our entire conversation, which was FINE with me.

He began to talk and said, "Jessie, I don't want to take you to jail today."

I responded, "Then don't."

He stated, "If you come with me to the state prosecutor's office and tell us everything you know about Marco, we will drop your charges."

My response was simple, "Take me to jail."

Well, off I went. It was a first. The officers handcuffed me and put me in the back seat of the police car while I made small talk with them. I was trying to make the best of the situation by not thinking about it. On the way to jail, I found myself fiddling with the handcuffs. I was only about 115 pounds then and I am 5'9', with highly skinny wrists. You might think I'm about to tell you I slipped out of the handcuffs and jumped out the door. Well, I thought about it. I then thought again. I had nowhere to go and to get out of this situation the right way. So, I slipped the handcuff back over my wrist and sat quietly. We arrived at the jail, and the police officer helped me out of the car and walked me into booking. I had never seen anything like that place: The smell, the people, how cold it is. It is so cold that you must put your arms into your t-shirt to stay warm, and then they yell at you for putting your arms in your t-shirt. The grown women in single cells, one smashing her head on the window screaming.

Let us say it was a hell of an experience. I was stuck in booking for 3 hours. They finally came to take my mug shot. I wanted to let everyone know I was okay in there and could handle myself, so I ensured my mugshot reflected that. They must put the handcuffs back on you before they take you to get your mug shot. As the lady attempted to make the handcuffs tight enough for me not to get out, she realized she couldn't. It was comical, honestly. She tightened the handcuffs as tight as they would go, then pushed her head forward at me like she had no idea what to do next. I then slipped my hand right out of the handcuffs and waved at her. She thought it was hilarious (thank goodness) and quickly asked me to do it again and wave at her coworker across the room, so I did! She didn't end up zip-tying me. The waves made her trust me a little. She then took me into another room to get my picture taken. When they book you, they take everything on your body and make you change into their clothes. They took my damn hair tie. So, my hair was down and a mess! But I still smirked at the camera when getting my mug shot taken. It was so bad that they made me take another picture without smiling. I held my head up higher and smirked just a little less. That picture was my mug shot—the winner.

After taking my mugshot, they brought me back to booking to wait longer. They had given me a piece of paper with my charges on it. I decided to unfold it and see what I was up against. It wasn't good. They had charged me with all of Marcos's charges and then some. I had never had a first offense, and they gave me NO bond. It meant I could only be bonded out after my court hearing. The situation was terrifying, but why two years later? Finally, they got me and a few other women to be moved to the dorms. They took us into this warehouse-looking room with nothing but steel bunk beds and a TV mounted on the wall, too high up for anyone to reach. On the TV was a football game. They put on football games in a women's ward. What kind of hell was this? I settled in with no pillow, a sack over my thin mattress, and a non-existent sheet. Instead of putting the potato sack-looking thing over my bed, I got inside it. It was freezing. Then I used "the sheet" as a pillow and to put over my eyes to sleep, as they never turn off the lights and there is no clock to tell you what time of day it is. It's almost trippy losing track of time like that. There is no way of knowing if it's the middle of the day or the middle of the night. We would make phone calls to ask people what time it was.

In my dorm, about fifteen other women were there with me. I slept most of the time. On day one, I slept all day, as sleeping was better than my current reality. They tried to feed us, but it looked like dog food, and I was not about to hug those toilets. The guards wouldn't give the women pads or sanitary items, which showed in the bathrooms. Not wanting to catch Aids, I told myself I would not eat or drink. That way, I wouldn't have to go to the toilet, get sick, or use the bathroom. Boy, was that rough. On day two, I woke up to new inmates in my dorm—all prostitutes. There was a "sting" operation, and they were on the opposite end of it. They all got brought in together. Joleen was the "bottom bitch", which I later figured out means she was the leader. She was calm, not too loud, and lovely once she saw my charges. We started talking, and she explained to me that they did not have pimps. They called themselves "renegades," meaning they called all their shots. You learn something new every day, I thought. After talking to Joleen for a while, I decided to go back to sleep.

Then, she asked me, "Why aren't you using the phone?"

"Anyone I would call right now should be on the phone with someone else, trying to get me out of here," I replied.

She nodded with respect, and I rolled over and put my sheet over my face to shield the bright fluorescent lights above me. The prostitutes were talking amongst themselves (which helped me sleep because I usually sleep with the TV on) when the women in the bed in front of me started talking shit to them. Mind you, I'm coming off my antidepressants and bipolar medication, making me highly irritable, and I hate when people wake me up. I waited to see if the argument between this crazy lady and the prostitutes would die down, but it only got louder. I had enough, and I snapped. I jumped up out of my so-called bed and began to yell (more like a roar) and slam my hand on the bed.

"Shut the fuck up and look around!" I yelled to the crazy lady. "We are all in JAIL. Leave them alone!" Everyone was shocked because I was quiet and kept to myself most of the time.

The prostitutes started yelling, "Thug Jessie!" They were chanting as they threw their hands in the air. It was a relief because I didn't want to make them angry.

It was still day two, and now I couldn't go back to sleep because I got myself all worked up. There was a tiny, tiny girl in my dorm who seemed funny. She didn't seem like a drug addict or a prostitute, so I wondered what she was in for.

"What is YOUR name?" I asked.

She said, "BD."

"BD? What does that stand for?"

"Big dick." She replied.

I giggled. "Well, you can call me BP."

"Now, what does that stand for?" she asked.

I said, "Big Pimping."

We both laughed and continued to talk. It must have been nighttime because the rest of the dorm was sleeping while we were wasting time trying to talk to the guys in the dorm next to us. We were sick of watching football, so BD put me on her shoulders to reach the buttons to change the channel. She made my time in jail bearable. She was there on a RICO charge. We had the two worst charges in the dorm. People kept getting bonded out and getting to go home while we sat there with no bond, waiting on our first appearance to try and get a bond to get out. After goofing off all night, they called about nine girls to come for their first appearance. I was one of those girls. They put all nine of us in a room the size of a small bathroom. We were on top of each other, and we all smelled. No showers were where we were, and they didn't provide deodorant.

We were in that room for 3 hours before anyone got called. They treated us like animals. Eventually, though, names started to get called. Then, the door opened, and they said my name. I got up, squeezed through the girls, and saw an attorney standing with the police officer. He was MY attorney and had spoken with the judge about my bond. He did it! I got a bond. I could go home. If my family could afford it, that is. They then sent me back to the dorm to wait to be bonded out. I slept for I don't know how long before the other girls returned from their first appearance, including my new friend. She came back into the dorm crying, so I went to find out what had happened. She didn't get seen because the judge ran out of time, so she would have to wait until next week to try to get a bond. I felt horrible for her; she was hysterical, and I wanted to hug her, but I was on day three and smelled like onions. She said she didn't mind, so I gave her a smelly hug. I let her be for a while and went back to sleep, hoping to wake up to get bonded out. Well, it worked!

I woke up to a guard yelling, "HAYS!"

"Yes," I replied. I jumped up, grabbed my stuff, and said goodbye to my friend.

I walked with the guard for what felt like forever down the most extended hallway. They returned all my clothes and wedding ring, but not my phone, as they had a warrant to search it, which was fine. It was just a bunch of pictures of kittens and kids, nothing terrible. Now I was just out of a phone (thanks a lot, cops). So, I got dressed, put my ring back on, and then was escorted to where people got picked up. I immediately saw my mom, husband, and kids waiting for me. I couldn't believe it! I missed them so much! I gave them the biggest hugs ever! We all got in the car, and they took me to get something to eat, as it had been three days since I had eaten or drank anything. I lost at least six pounds.

We were driving home after grabbing some fast food when my husband told me he had a HUGE surprise for me when I got home. I was excited, not knowing what it could be, but he exaggerated it. We get home, and it seems unreal. I missed my family and my home so much. I was extremely grateful to be home (BEFORE THE FIGHTS CAME ON THAT SATURDAY). I settled in and took a much-needed shower, and then Marco wanted to show me his surprise. I follow him to our room, where he starts to dig under the bed, looking for something. As I watch, he pulls out this enormous bag full of marijuana—about three pounds of it.

I immediately freaked out and told him, "Get it OUT of my house! I just got out of jail! And I'm not trying to go back."

"Ok, ok!" he replied.

What a gift, huh? Marco eventually calmed me down, and I ignored the issue. We ended up watching the fights, and I slept better than I had in my entire life. My lovely, comfortable mattress topper and pillow were bliss. But I could not deny the feeling in my gut that this was not over; this was another new beginning. I got out of jail in time to return to work without missing, but that one day. My boss was BEYOND understanding. She told me to go to my classroom. I thought I would immediately be sent out with my kids. I was still unsure that my job was secure. It felt like I would get fired any moment once they looked up my charges. I made it through day one, but the next day, I came in, and they asked me for my driver's license. I knew this was it. I was losing my job, and my kids would have to leave their private education. I went to class with my heart pounding. I managed to get my class in order, all sitting and waiting to read our morning book and go over the days of the week. The day continued. Towards the end of the day, I got pulled into the manager's office, a manager who loved me and I had the utmost respect. She sat me down and explained that I was no longer allowed to work with children and could no longer work there. I began to cry and told her I understood completely. She apologized and said there would always be a spot for me once everything worked out. I thanked her and left the room to get my kids from their after-school class. They saw me and asked why we were leaving, and I had to tell them that we were no longer returning to the private Elementary school. They started to cry, which made me cry again, and we all three walked to the car crying. We loved that school. It was a home away from home; my kids got a fantastic education, and I was there if they needed anything. That was no longer the case. Public school, here they come. Now, just because I was out of jail didn't mean I was off the hook. It just meant I was out until my trial date, when they would decide whether I would be charged. It meant I was out on bond. It was this level of uncertainty that gave me the worst anxiety and a sense of always being overwhelmed. Also, I did not know how they would charge my husband. Were my kids going to have parents? Would they arrest me again? What were we going to do?

16

The Cats

Amid all those incidents, my cat Simba got pregnant because I never got her spayed. This is relevant, I promise. As the days passed and we waited to hear from our attorneys, Simba kept getting bigger. During Christmas that year, Lexi was in the hospital, and I stayed with her the entire time. She inherited my asthma and allergies, which makes it easy for us to get sick, especially at that time of the year. We celebrated Christmas on December 27th when Lexi got home from the hospital. She was such a good sport as she waited to open her gifts.

When we got home from the hospital, I couldn't find Simba anywhere, and she always would come when I called for her. I looked everywhere and eventually made and posted flyers around the neighborhood, thinking she had gone outside. We heard nothing from the flyers for a few days, and we still couldn't find her around the house. Then, one day, Lexi and Lucy were looking for a tape measurer for Marco, and Lexi happened to look under the recliner on the sofa. Sure enough, there was a black and white kitten that Lexi pulled out from underneath the couch. She thought it was a sock, but Simba had been hiding under the sofa having her baby the whole time we were looking for her. We decided to keep the kitten and name him Mickey. He was the cutest little thing, and guess what? He stayed small. They are called munchkin cats. He was also a little slow, not the brightest, but super cute and sweet. I thought his size was strange. So, I started to do some research on small cats to see if it was a real thing, as he wasn't getting any taller. I discovered that munchkin cats were huge in China but rare in the United States. That gave me an idea to breed him. My mom and my husband hated the idea. They thought it would be unsuccessful and we would get stuck with many cats, but I tried to prove them wrong. With the felonies on my record, it was impossible to get a job. I had to figure out something, and I thought this was it. Simba had another litter. I thought I could sell them for a low price, like $300, not realizing I had $1,200 kittens that people would love to buy. You would be surprised to know the number of people looking for a specific cat breed. Everyone is too busy breeding dogs. I was going to start my own business. And it worked until my stud (Mickey) ran away. And not being the smartest, I'm sure he couldn't find his way home. We put out flyers again, but nothing.

17

Oh, Bond!

Everything was going as well as possible, considering my husband and I were still out on bond. Marco still wanted to make me the happiest girl in the world, so he saved his money and bought me a new ring. We got married in 2020, but we couldn't afford expensive rings because we were in the process of being evicted at that time. Therefore, I purchased a sterling silver ring online for $77. It was perfect for me. I didn't need some big fancy ring to feel loved by him, but he needed an actual engagement ring. So, he got one. One morning in February, he woke me up with both kids, and then he got down on one knee with a bouquet and a ring and asked me to marry him. It was everything I ever wanted, and the ring was stunning. I knew he worked so hard to buy it for me to see my face and make me happy. I was smitten! It made the fact that we might not be together much longer hurt even worse. However, it was inevitable.

For Lexi's sixth birthday, we went to SeaWorld. She wanted to go there for her birthday, so we made it happen. We invited a couple of friends, including Lexi's kindergarten teacher. She was awesome! Her name is Ms. Mac. She met us there at 10:00 am, and we began our adventures. Ms. Mac suggested we get a beer, and there was no way I could say no to Lexi's teacher. So, we got beers, and from there, I continued to drink. We had a fabulous day! It was 6:00 pm when we were finally wrapping it up. By that time, I was shit-faced. The kids were on their last ride on Elmo Street, and Marco said he had to go to the bathroom. I suggested he go before the kids got off the ride so we could leave immediately. He agreed, and off he went. When he left, I saw a security guard cornered and ganged up by about fifteen people.

In my drunken state, I thought, "WORLD STAR!" So, I pulled out the video camera on my phone. Once I hit the record button, the flash turned on. My drunken ass forgot to turn it off before I started to record. Wonderful job, Jess. One of the girls in the group saw me from my apparent shiny light. She saw it and immediately ran up to me, took my phone out of my hands, and pushed me. Now I'm wasted, and all I'm thinking is how I will get my phone back. I'm not a short person, and neither was she. So, I reached up to grab the phone that she was holding over her head.

She pulled back and said, "What will you do about it?"

Famous last words! I balled up my left hand and began to beat the girl like I was fighting for my life. Let's be honest: with how drunk I was, I was fighting for my life. Both of my kids were now behind me. Lucy later told me that I had hit the girl about six times with my left hand, and I was about to hit her with my right as I had her in between my legs. However, when I pulled my right hand back, someone grabbed it. I immediately thought it was Marco, but when I turned around, it was another girl. I thought I was getting jumped. So, instead of hitting the girl underneath me, I swung my elbow back and hit the girl who grabbed my hand three times in her face. That was the last time I saw her. I looked down and saw that the girl I was fighting before had gotten up. I looked over, and there was a pile of men on top of my husband, including the girl I was initially fighting. Now, the men I could do nothing about, but that bitch I could grab off him. I ran up to the pile that was on top of my husband, pulled the girl down, and put her in a headlock. I didn't hit her. I just held her in place so she couldn't jump back in. Then, before I knew it, Marco threw all the men off him like a lion attacked by a clan of hyenas! It was wild! Once Marco was up and finally let go of one of the guys, I let go of the girl and ran over to him and the kids, who were being watched by a lovely family who saw the whole thing.

Lucy yelled, "MOM, YOU DIDN'T GET HIT ONCE!".

I was still in shock at what had just happened, and now cops were starting to talk to us. Oh no! We were both out on bond and fucked if we got in trouble for this or any trouble for that matter. They sat us away from each other and began to question us both separately. But I did have that video on my phone, which was enough proof that we did not start the fight. The security guards took our side and got us out before statements were made. They grabbed our kids, who were then being watched by police officers and escorted us to their van to drive us to our car. They saved our asses that night. Thank you, Frank, if you're reading this!

When I was arrested (at the school, not for the fight), Marco agreed to the seven-year plea deal only if my charges were dropped. They said that the seven-year plea deal was no longer on the table, and the only offer available for him now would be for him to serve 15 years, and they would drop my charges. He then read my discovery (all the evidence against me) because I was too scared to read it myself. His face said it all. He told me my discovery was worse than his. They had a whole handprint of mine on a bag of weed in the safe, allegedly. The charges and the discovery were so bad I just began to cry. Being the man that my husband is, he saved me and took the 15 years. He said the children had to have a parent, and that parent needed to be me. How soul-crushing, devastating, all the words!

I was so heartbroken that I had to up my anti-depressant medication. Marco had a month from taking the plea deal to resolve his affairs and say goodbye to us. That month, he quit his job to spend time with us—every minute of every day. We did everything we could together, and he got to be there for Lucy's birthday. Since he quit, we didn't have much money to spare. Marco wanted to take Lucy out for her birthday, so he sold his car. That's something she will never forget.

She asks me, "Can he adopt me from prison?" "When is he going to come home?" "Why is he leaving?" All questions were tough to answer.

My answer for most of them was, "I will explain when you're older."

I had to tell her the truth about the time and how long he would be gone. Therefore, Marco and I sat Lucy down because she was older and understood better and told her how long he would be away. She was devastated and started to cry hysterically. We both tried to comfort her and explained we have an attorney to file an appeal (filing a motion for a lower sentence or no sentence at all). That made her feel better, but we still knew how hurt she was.

18

Farewell

The day before Marco turned himself in, I invited all his closest friends to our house to say goodbye and spend time with him before he left. We let the kids stay up late that night to spend as much time as possible with him. I invited a lot of people, and some of them arrived early. Some were gang members, some drug dealers, and some ordinary people with hard-working jobs. But they all had one thing in common: Marco. They all showed up for him, every single one of them. Knowing that all these people loved Marco was a bittersweet feeling, yet we were about to watch him turn himself in. We all hung out, we laughed, and we cried. It was a very emotional night. Well, night turned into morning. I didn't want to go to sleep and miss a minute of my time with my husband. We stayed up all night together, and so did our friends and family. Eventually, the time had come to go to the courthouse. Our friend, Lisa, came to pick us up because I knew I couldn't drive after what I was about to witness. We said goodbye to the friends who stayed with us until that moment, and then we got into the truck with Lisa. It was a quiet drive to the courthouse, as we were all in despair. Marco sat in the back seat with me, and I held his hand the entire car ride and cuddled him as we both cried. I cried the whole time! There wasn't a moment that I was okay. Those last moments in Marco's arms were the moments I will cherish forever. He is my soulmate, my twin flame, as some would say. I don't care what we have been through. He had grown into the best husband, father, and son-in-law anyone could ask for. He was very present and involved with our little family. From taking the kids for ice cream to letting them ride him around like a "horsie." He made our dinner every night after a hard day of work and always did It with a smile. It was these things I was going to miss the most about him, not to mention his big, strong arms wrapped around me in bed. We arrived at the courthouse and slowly got out of the car. As we walked in, we were met by both of our attorneys (we couldn't have the exact attorney due to a conflict of interest), and they were quick to shake Marco's hand, knowing that what he was doing was incredible. He was turning himself in for 15 years to save me from going to prison myself. Our attorneys also advised us that if we were to spend just one night in jail/prison at the same time, we would lose all rights to our children. That was something we could not take a chance on. Marco knew that, and that is why he took the 15 years.

We walked into the courtroom: Lisa, Marco, and me. I was still sobbing my eyes out, if not more so than before. The judge called his name and asked him to come to the front. That was the last time I touched Marco and felt him breathe, and he was gone. He pled guilty and was sentenced to 15 years in prison. They handcuffed him, wearing a suit and tie. He left the room with his head held high. He left the room, and I cried harder, hugging Lisa. It had to be one of the worst days of my life. My nightmare had become a reality. I will never forget that moment when I lost half of myself. It was gone. I felt this emptiness that ate me alive, this pain in my chest that felt like he had been physically removed from me. It was awful and overpowering.

The time had come to leave the courtroom without Marco. I walked out with Lisa on my arm and my attorneys behind me. We walked out of the courthouse this way, silent. Wanting to yell at our attorneys for letting something like this happen after all the money our friends and family had put into them. However, what would that help at this point? It just stirred up more emotions to deal with, so I kept quiet. We reached the parking garage and shook hands respectfully, and I walked away with Lisa. We walked to the truck, and she consoled and got me in. She drove me home, where I cried the rest of the day.

19

Layla! And The New Fight

I was on the phone with my best friend, Layla, daily. We became friends when the circumstances unfolded, and she never left my side. She would call and talk to me for hours every day about anything and everything to ensure I was okay. She was the only person who understood how I felt because she had been in a similar situation. My kitten business was booming, so we would always go out to eat and vibe at the beach with our kids. It was a great distraction from my current reality. No Marco! It was great to know that I had a friend like Layla around, who always called to check on me, dropped anything she was doing if I needed her, and just talking to her on the phone alone helped me so much. She was always there for me, no matter what, just like she promised. I have no idea how I would have gotten through the situation without her. The pool and the beach were our happy places. We frequently went to the pool where my mother worked, lounging in the Florida sun. Once, we rented a hotel room on the beach for Layla's birthday (before I was approved to see Marco). It was gorgeous! We had so much fun, going on the beach at night with the kids and flashlights to look for crabs and having a few nighttime drinks to end the night. It was a fantastic time, great for my mental well-being, as I was still highly heartbroken over Marco and confused about how we would get him out. Layla helped me through the contemplation daily. She was my best friend. Not only was she generous and genuine, but she was also strong and independent. Layla was a single mother with her own house and a Dodge Durango. She provided extensively for her family. She was so strong it came off borderline intimidating, but not to me. She was always so sweet to me that she didn't intimidate me at all. If anything, I felt safe around her. She helped me get through the next phase of my life.

We were filing for an appeal (where you re-open a case for another chance to go to trial or get your sentence reduced). Unfortunately, we had to wait until January 20th, 2024, to file it because my statute of limitations was up then. After this date, they could no longer re-open my case for any reason. When you file for an appeal, it re-opens your case. If they re-opened Marco's case, it would also re-open mine, as our cases had been consolidated. That meant we had to wait until that date to file the appeal to keep me safe. I apologize for the legal jargon. It will help you understand eventually. Marco turned himself in May of 2023, and I couldn't see him for five months until they approved my application.

Eventually, they approved my visitation request form, and I could go with the kids to see him. On our first visit, Lucy was nervous, as she better understood where she was than Lexi did.

On the other hand, Lexi couldn't have been more excited as she ran up and down the hallways yelling, "DADDY!"

Of course, we had to go through the process of signing in, being searched, and counting any jewelry or hair ties we had on us. They finally let us into the visitation room to see him. He wasn't out yet. The room was full of men in blue, talking to their families across the table. It was a big, square room with plastic tables and chairs. They had a bin of cards, coloring books, dominoes, and board games to play with the kids, which was cool. We played Uno while waiting for Marco. You had to follow specific rules while visiting an inmate, such as only a hello, a goodbye kiss, and one hug, and you had to sit on the opposite side of the table as the inmate unless you were a child. They were lenient regarding these rules, as I got lots of hugs and kisses without any issues. Marco came out and into the visitation room, and my heart stopped. I missed him and his touch and his stupid jokes so much. We ran up to him and gave him the biggest group hug ever! We were so happy to be back in his arms, even for a moment. We sat at the table and caught up before getting food.

Now, I mean prison food, what they would sell to the inmates who had money in their accounts from friends and family. It was alright; they had honey buns and chicken sandwiches. That's what I always got: the chicken sandwich. The girls got ramen, and I bought Marco whatever his little heart desired. We were allowed to bring in $50 and no bills larger than $20. It was enough to feed us all and stuff Marco silly. I wanted to make sure he was well fed, as I had seen firsthand what they fed you in jail, and it was disgusting. I wouldn't eat it. So, I always ensured he had money in his books for food and fed him well every Saturday and Sunday during visitation. Our first visit went terrific. It was so awesome to see and touch him, watch him with the kids, and be so present even in jail (he had not been moved to prison yet). Since then, we had a visitation scheduled for every weekend. That's what we did: visit Daddy. We would always leave happy and full. The best part of my week was going with the girls to see him. We went every weekend for about two months, as it was super close to my house, about a 30-minute drive. That made it very convenient to see him on both days of the weekend. Remember that this was not Marcos's permanent residence; he was still in jail while waiting to be moved to his permanent facility.

I get his phone call after being spoiled and seeing Marco every weekend. He sounded upset, and this time, he called from a different phone number. He explained that they had moved him to his permanent facility that morning, which was not nearby. It was 6 hours away in Panama City, right by Alabama. Being that I lived in Central Florida with two kids made it almost impossible to see him now. It was devastating. How was I going to get through the years only getting to see him when I had the money? I never had money to spare between two kids and rent. However, at one point, Lisa surprised me with a two-day rental house next to Marco's prison. I was so excited! I could not wait to leave.

I began packing my bags as Lexi looked at me and said, "Mom, we only need one outfit a day." Implying that I was packing too much.

"I know, honey!" I laughed as I continued to over pack.

I had just gotten a new car, so we took it on its first road trip. We were finally on the road and on our way to see my husband: Me, Lisa, Lexi, and Lucy. We made it there before dark, and it was beautiful. The rental sat on a farm surrounded by cows and horses. The cabin-like house had two bedrooms and four beds; it was perfect. Not only would I get to see my husband, but it also felt like a vacation. I loved Lisa. Going with her made it feel like that much more of a vacation. She was fun and full of life. She was the mother of my best friend, Pipp. Tragically, Pipp was murdered at an early age before we had time to grow up. Marco had become best friends with her family while she was alive and after she passed away. See, Marcos's first real girlfriend was Pipp; that's how I knew him, Pippa's boyfriend. I think she would be happy that he ended up with me, not someone who would take advantage of him. I am someone who would love him unconditionally and never forget her.

On our first night at the cabin, we explored and put our stuff away, then headed to Walmart to grab snacks, things for dinner, and firewood for the fire pit. At Walmart, I noticed everyone around me had sores on their faces and arms. Anywhere visible, there were sores. Usually, this is a sign of meth abuse. There was nothing to do there besides drugs.

We got our stuff quickly and kept an eye out, walking to the car. We decided to get breakfast stuff and snacks, as we would be eating with Marco, and we stopped and got pizza for dinner.

We got home and ate; then Lucy wanted to play with Lisa's ghost-hunting kit. It was a bad idea with Lexi around as she got terrified and started to say she wanted to go home now. It was adorable, but I felt terrible. She was scared and didn't want to be here anymore. Suddenly, we heard a big thud. I said it was time to go inside and pushed Lexi through the door! Lucy wanted to wait for Lisa to get her iPad off the stand. I'm sure it was nothing, but better safe than sorry. My first thought was, "meth head." We went inside and started to get ready for bed. Lexi was so scared of the "ghosts" that she slept on the couch in the same bedroom as me and Lisa. Lucy slept on the couch because she was afraid and wanted to sleep with a TV. Lisa and I woke up to Lexi sleeping in the middle of our bed, pushing us both off each end. We eventually go ahead and get up and make coffee and some bagels. Visitation started at 9:00 am, and we wanted to be the first ones there, and we were. Thanks to Lexi's sleeping habits (she always sleeps with me).

We left the house early and were only 15 minutes away from Marco's prison. Finding the prison took us a while because the entrance differed from the map. Eventually, we found it and checked in. We went through the process of searching and counting things before being let into the visitation room. Once we were at the door, it was locked, but it had a small window on it, and I could see Marco sitting there by himself. I hated seeing him all alone, and I couldn't do anything but bang on the window to get the guard's attention to let us into the room. It worked. They noticed us and let us in to see him! Oh my gosh, were we all so happy and excited! Lisa and I had brought in $50 each to eat and stuff Marco. We played games, joked around, and caught up. It was a blast to be with him, even if it was in prison. He looked amazing; you could tell he had been working out. He had gained about forty pounds of muscle, given that all he can do is work out. I loved it, but I wished it were under different circumstances.

We left when they closed visitation, which was at 3 pm. We stayed the entire time they allowed for visitation, and we needed more. We left, returned to the car, and returned to the rental. We had visitation again the next day, so we stayed another night. We returned to the rental and decided that night to make a bonfire, play more ghost games (Lucy was obsessed), get in our jammies, and watch a scary movie. We bought firewood at Walmart the night before to make the bonfire and already had our ghost-hunting stuff out. We had a great night; it was relaxing, spooky, and fun all at the same time. We went to bed early to get up early in the morning to see Marco. We were up early the next day, ready to see Marco again. Unfortunately, this was our last day before we headed home, and we needed to arrive on time. It gave me horrible anxiety, but eventually, we made it, and I got to hold Marco in my arms again. After 3 pm, we all cried, knowing it would be a while before we saw him again. It was expensive to stay in Panama City for a weekend with two kids, so we could only return once we could afford it.

20

Head Above Water

I was still selling my kittens, ones I would find online for free (Siamese, Russian Blues, and Ragdolls), and re-home them. The profit helped with rent and bills and made it so Layla and I could go out to dinner and our favorite little hole-in-the-wall bar afterward. We had dinner about once a week and the beach every other weekend with our kids. Her son, Ezekiel, was 14 years old but was terrific with children. He was always all over the place, being a big goofball and playing with Lexi and Lucy. They had a blast together and got along well. It was a plus to our friendship. One day, we were lying at the pool overlooking the beach when I noticed Layla and her boyfriend having the best time together. I was so happy for her but simultaneously so sad for myself. It wasn't her fault at all. I was missing my husband. I started crying and tried to hide it, but Layla quickly noticed it. She walked over, scooped me up, and sat there while I cried. I didn't want to ruin our little vacation, but she didn't make it seem like I did. She just comforted me and told me everything was going to be okay. I quickly calmed down, and I had her to thank for it. She was by far the best friend I had.

Eventually, summer ended, and our beach days were postponed. We also had to cut down on our dinners because I had financial issues. See, my mom paid for everything. She had a very high-paying job, allowing her to care for the four of us. We still struggled, even with my kitten business. I felt horrible putting all my responsibilities on her, but I could not get a job unless my charges were expunged, which was expensive to do, and I didn't have the money to do it. My charges were bad: armed trafficking of cocaine over four hundred grams and possession of pounds of weed. No one would hire me, not even Walmart, for the overnight shift. That's why my kitten business was so important.

When Simba had her munchkin kittens, they started to make me money. My munchkin left the house and never returned when it was going well. Poor thing couldn't defend itself to save its life. I was devastated. My favorite cat was gone, and my business ended. He was my only stud, and these cats cost a lot. I was pushed over the edge with defeat. Marco is so far away in prison, my business is over, I cannot make rent without my kittens, and the list continues. I didn't know what to do besides cry.

Trying to produce a solution, I did what I always do and ran to my mom. I also looked on my kitten site for a munchkin to see if I could find one for a reasonable price before running to Mom. I explained to her that if we didn't invest in a new stud, we wouldn't be able to make rent. She saw my look and knew I was teeter-tottering on the edge of a breakdown, so she said yes to getting me the new REAL deal munchkin stud. She pulled money from her 401K to do so. I felt horrible, but I knew I would make it up to her with the amount of money this cat would make me. My mom was my everything. I couldn't imagine my life without her. I would be homeless with two kids, having these charges on my record. She saved my life, and it's my life goal to make her proud and be able to take care of her for once. Now, I just needed as many unspayed females as I could manage.

I reverted to social media, looking for kittens to sell or keep and start breeding. Well, I found both, luckily. I had already had an unspayed female ragdoll with papers, Simba, who started this whole thing, and my Siamese Munchkin, Meeko, who would make this entire thing happen. He was only four months old then but would mature and make things happen soon enough. As time passed, I adopted two small female bobtails, one all-black named Doja and one named Toriti. But none of the female cats were getting pregnant? Why? Come to find out, Meeko's legs were too short to "do the deed." Funny, but disappointing. He tried his best, but he just physically could not do it. So, I decided to keep Meeko and get a Ragdoll stud. Back to social media, I went! I found a beautiful bi-colored, long-haired Ragdoll for free, about two hours away. I immediately went to get him and kept his original name, Wybee. He was the sweetest cat ever! I couldn't have gotten luckier. Not fixed and a teenager. It was perfect. Well, as soon as I get him, my four cats go into heat (meaning they are ready to get pregnant), and I watch Meeko continue to try. Wybee didn't try at all, given his age; he was still an adolescent. Meeko ended up getting Simba and Doja pregnant! I was so happy and proud all at once. He did it! These kittens were going to save our asses. My cats began to grow more prominent, and I fed them kitten food because it had more calcium. It was better for the babies and helped with bone development. They were doing great!

21

Loneliness

I spoke to Marco around 2 to 3 times daily over the phone. We would talk about the kids, our days, and anything interesting. In the state of Florida, there are no conjugal visits. Meaning that we couldn't have sex while he was serving a 15-year sentence. It was harder than I imagined, but I remained loyal, hoping the underway appeal would lower his sentence to something more reasonable. One day, I called Marco's attorney to see the appeal status. He told me the prosecutors could not suppress any evidence because everything they found was usable, and they had the correct warrant. I had no heart to tell Marco about this. He was in prison. The last thing I wanted to do was be the reason he felt defeated. The good news is that his attorney represented the detective on our case, which is a conflict of interest. The attorney said he would draft a new plea deal with a lesser sentence and file a motion to get the judge's approval. He said it would take three years or less to get done, but it was improbable to be approved. I was riddled with anxiety and depression. I had started to take anti-depressant medications about a year prior, but they were no longer getting the job done. I had been through so many horrible experiences that anxiety and depression overrode my medication.

I started to talk to my doctor about either switching or upping my dosage of medication. She thought it would be best to switch me, which would cause me to spiral, but eventually feel much better. It's weird how that works. I was worried because it already felt like I was spiraling, and I didn't want it to get worse. I had to make sure my long-term mental health was in check, especially being a mom of two. So, I decided to make the switch and endure two weeks of suffering for long-term results. I jumped from one medication to two different ones. My doctor thought it was necessary, given my situation.

22

Vee

My friend, Vee, was there for me often during that time. I had been friends with her for over ten years. We met when we worked at the same strip club and lived in the same neighborhood. Now, before your minds begin to wander, I was NOT a stripper, and neither was Vee. I was a cocktail server, and Vee was my bartender. She would make the drinks. I would bring them to the dirty older men, gawking over those naked women. Vee had the better end of the stick at that place, behind a bar and away from the men sitting on the stage. Working there was quite an experience. It was a whole different world in there. Everyone there did drugs. I dabbled in some Adderall (keep in mind I was still in my early twenties and working until 3 am) to stay awake during my shifts and make me more talkative, but I never messed around with anything else there. I was too scared. The place was a shit hole, and I could only imagine the drugs were shit too. Vee was the same way and didn't do the drugs by which we were surrounded. We became close, so much so they had to separate us. Eventually, we found out that we lived 2 minutes away from each other, making us inseparable. We began to carpool and hang out after work every night. We used to just stay up and talk all night. It was so much fun at the time. However, after a while, the strip club environment began to get to me a little bit. One night at work, someone got shot and killed by the security guard in front of the club. The police kept us inside the club that night until 5 am. No one could come or go from the establishment. It was an extraordinarily long night and terrifying all at the same time. The security guard who shot the man who surprisingly wasn't holding a gun got taken to jail for murder. The other guy had nothing to defend himself with, which turned the case into a murder case. The entire time that we were locked in there, I hung out with Vee. Bullshitted, trying to distract ourselves from what was going on outside.

Eventually, Marco paid me to quit working at the club. He came to visit me one night when we first started dating, and he hated it. He felt I was being degraded and offered to pay me more than what I made, on average, weekly. I took him up on his offer. Through quitting, I remained best friends with Vee. We went through thick and thin together from her shitty relationships to my abusive ones. She saw the hell that Marco put me through while I was pregnant with his daughter Lexi but always supported me no matter what happened. She continued to bartend until she met her boyfriend, who had a lot of money to spare. Vee had always paid for her condominium, all three of her kids, and any and every expense otherwise. She never needed a man. She always took care of herself and her family.

One day, Vee got sick with breast cancer, something her mother had passed away from. It was terrifying. I couldn't imagine not having her with me, but I knew she was a fighter and would get through this. And I was right; she made it through and went into remission. She made it through all three times of having stage 4 breast cancer. I was at the hospital with her as much as possible, trying to take her mind off things. Which I'm sure was impossible, given she had cancer. The fact that her beautiful mother passed away from it always made it that much scarier. The situation also brought us closer, and I never wanted to leave her side again! We always stayed close, even if it was just over the phone, while we lived our busy lives filled with children and chaos. She was my rock. One time, while I was pregnant, Marco started reaching out to my friends to tell them anything I had told him, hoping to get a response from them regarding me. He was looking for "dirt" to prove I wasn't a good person. One of those people was Vee. She told him to kick rocks, no matter what he said or any threat he made. She had nothing to tell him at the time anyway, nothing he didn't already know. But he felt that she did. She wasn't scared of him and stayed out of it. Right then and there, I knew I could tell her anything. Anything!

23

The End Of The Begining

Marco is still in prison in Panama City, and I am still lonely and depressed. I started to focus on selling my kittens and making money. I won't even mention how much money I made, but it was enough to help support us significantly and pay for the things the kids needed. I loved assisting kittens while waiting for the litter. It made me a remarkable amount of money, and I knew the litter my cat produced would put me on top. At one point, I could not wait for the two litters I had due because the rent was due also. So, I went online and found four Ragdoll kittens for $100. That was nothing compared to what I would sell them for, but I had to wait until they were old enough for me to pick them up. Once I got the baby Ragdolls, they sold within the first week, and that paid for rent and a partial car insurance payment.

I will not know what will happen to Marco for about another year. That's around how long it takes to have a trial date set after the appeal is filed. I am startled about the unknown, our futures left in someone else's hands, and the emptiness of missing my other half. I now have enough money to visit him with the kids and Lisa again. Lisa's husband also got approved for the visitation, so he may come with us (if he can stand us).

I started to draft this book as therapy for my everyday life. It eventually turned into what you just read, something deep and personal, and I chose to share it with you—the raw pieces of me that no one knew besides my closest friends and family. I decided to share it with the world. I'm sure I will be judged, but that's okay. Different people will think different things, and that's more of a reason why I want to tell my story. So, there you have it, this is my story. It may be sad, but it's mine. Allegedly!

About The Author

"I love and live for my children; they are my entire world. I have made some mistakes in the past (big ones). Still, my children never gave up, and neither did I. I have learned the hard way how to behave in society, but I can proudly say that I am now in a fantastic place in my life. Finally, I have found myself. Writing is my passion, which is why I majored in English. I have gone through a lot in my life and have learned a lot from it. I grew up without my father. He left when I was one year old, and it's been me and my mother ever since. I have no siblings, so we were and are still incredibly close. My circumstances have made me stronger than I ever thought I could be. I want everyone to know you can be just as strong, no matter the situation."

www.ingramcontent.com/pod-product-compliance
Lightning Source LLC
Chambersburg PA
CBHW070445170726
48291CB00005B/1612